CIRCUS

CIRCUS

L'TANYA LEONE

Leone Press

Published by Leone Press

ISBN: 978-1-4792-9440-4

Typesetting services by BOOKOW.COM

I always glimpse over the dedications before I read a book, but now I see why authors give shout outs to those who walked with them through their writing pain.

To my mom Annie Mae who actually read the book (Just like a true mom): Who always believed in me even when I wasn't ready.

To my sister Michelle: No matter how many ideas I came up with, she was right there with me planning, scheming, and plotting.

Asa and Tana loved living in their small town called Seward, and most of all they enjoyed going to their favorite park. Only there was one teeny weeny problem in the park. It was at the edge of the woods watching and waiting for them to come closer.

Follow the exciting adventures of four kids who are running for their lives from someone or something that is determined to catch them at all cost.

You just might never go to a park again!

CHAPTER 1

Basil: Oh hi there. Are you here to see what is going on with Tana and Asa? Well, hold on to your seats because you are in for a good story. Listen closely, and you will see why you just might be afraid of playgrounds. Oh, you are wondering who I am? Well, I will tell you later because there is no time for introductions, and I just don't feel like it right now. Things will be happening today, and I just want you to sit back and relax. That's right sit back, relax, and enjoy the ride. I dare you.

"Pssst, pssst, Asa. Are you there?" asked Tana. Asa did not answer his little sister. He knew she would continue to bug him no matter how he responded to her. Asa could tell his sister was really mad because she was practically hissing on the other side of the door.

"If you won't answer me I'm leaving!" Tana yelled from the other side of the door.

Although he heard his big mouth sister, Asa continued staring at himself in the mirror. He wanted to make sure he looked good when they leave for the playground. He was determined Tana was not going to rush him again. The last time she made him rush out of the house he had toilet paper hanging from his foot, and everybody laughed at him. Asa was never so humiliated. It was so bad he turned tail and ran back home until he could not hear the laughter from the park anymore. The beating sound of his sister banging the bathroom door just made him take his time. Boy his sister could drive him nuts.

Asa always thought girls were so silly, and they were always giggling and whispering. He could not stand girls only a year ago. But now that's all he could think about, and he could not explain why. Mom said it is because he is growing older, and he is becoming more handsome, as each year passes. Then again Asa thought, only his mom thought he was good looking. As he looked in the mirror, he finally realized he was not as good looking as Pumpkin, the kid who all the girls swooned over at school. Asa sighed and told himself he was just as good looking as Pumpkin. Besides, mom said so. Tana's banging on the door made him remember they were going to the park, and so he had to stop daydreaming.

"Okay, okay! I'm ready," said Asa.

When Asa opened the door Tana was beside herself with anger. She could not understand what her brother could be doing in the bathroom. As Tana looked at her brother from head to toe, all she saw was a boy with skinny legs and a big head. For the last year Tana noticed her brother was really staying in that bathroom for a long time, and she could not for the life of her guess why. This is why she hated having to share a connected bathroom with her brother.

Thank goodness she had her own room, and most of all thank goodness mom and dad bought a house with separate rooms. Tana could not imagine sharing a room with him. Even though she loved her brother there were times she just wanted to strangle him. When Asa finally stepped out of the bathroom into her room, Tana looked him over from head to toe, and all she saw was a nerd.

"Ugh! Why are you wearing those crazy sneakers? Sheesh! Never mind, just hurry up before mom changes her mind and comes up with more chores for us to do," said Tana.

They both ran to Tana's door and peeked outside the room looking both ways down the hallway. Sister and brother looked at each other and smiled because there was no sign of mom and dad. Once they saw the coast was clear they sneaked over to the top of the staircase. Tana turned towards Asa and whispered.

"Don't step on that creaky step going down the stairs," Tana warned.

Asa thought his sister could be so bossy sometimes, but what could he do?

"Are you ready to run down?" asked Tana.

"Just go Tana!" exclaimed Asa.

Both kids leaped over the creaky top step and ran down the stairs. Tana barreled down the stairs running with Asa close behind her. 'Whew', Tana thought. They finally made it to the bottom of the stairs without a sound. Tana crept to the front door with Asa breathing down her neck. Tana thought Asa forgot to brush his teeth again because his breath was killing her. Oh well she thought, but there was no time for them to stand there and argue about stink breath. All Tana knew was she had some serious play time to do at the park. Plus all her friends Angie and Pee Wee were waiting for her. Tana gently opened the front door slowly. As she turned the knob, all she heard was the old door squeaking. Hearing that loud noise they both ran out the door slamming it shut laughing all the way down the sidewalk.

"Whew, Bababa boy that was close! I thought for sure mom was going to grab us at the door!" as Asa laughed with glee.

"You're lucky seeing that you nearly tripped out the door! Come on! I want to get to the park before it gets dark. All the other kids will be there. I want to get on the new monkey bars and that scary looking slide! Did you see how high it is? Remember when Pauly reached the top of the slide and just kind of fell all the way down? Boy that was weird. It was like some invisible hand pushed him," Tana added with a nervous smile.

"I know, that was kind of spooky, and nobody saw it but us." Asa began laughing when he thought about that day when Pauly went head first down the slide. "Boy, did you see Pauly's face when he ran home crying like a screaming hyena?"

"I know everybody at school was talking about it for a whole week! I still laugh about it. I'm just glad it wasn't me," said Tana.

Tana and Asa chatted like they were the best of friends forgetting about who hogged the bathroom that morning. It was a nice, bright day, and all the kids were out and about heading for the park. Tana saw some of her friends heading in the same direction they were going; she felt really good, and she was excited to get to the park and have fun with her friends. Asa was finally ready to enjoy the park with his friends and meet some girls. Asa and Tana finally arrived at the park. It made them excited because they saw all their friends enjoying all the rides.

"Look Tana, everybody is at the park! We might never get a turn!" yelled Asa.

"Oh Asa, come on, stop whining. You go to the swings, and I will get on the merry go round," replied Tana.

Asa hated when Tana gave him orders, because he was the older brother and bigger than his sister. He knew Tana was looking out for him, but it still made him a little mad when she told him what to do. Asa realized that Tana knew he loved the swings. That's why he would give his favorite gym shorts away to have a swing set in their backyard. So, he ran over to the swings hoping to run into one of his buddies and decided he would go on the monkey bars later on. Well, as time went by, the day became a little cooler, and the clouds were setting in. Tana and Asa were so busy playing they did not notice the park was emptying out, and the playground was getting spooky dark. It was the kind of dark that makes a kid know they will be chewed out at home for being late. When the entire sky was gray and covered with eerie looking clouds only then Tana realized how late it was. She was having so much fun she completely forgot about the time.

"Oh monkey muffins! Mom and dad are going to ground us if we come in late again," said Tana. This thought started Tana looking for her brother. When she spotted him on the monkey bars she began to see they were the only kids in the park.

Basil: "Uh-oh, it's darky dark."

Tana was so beside herself about being out late she began chattering to herself. If anyone saw her they would think she was stone crazy.

"Now I know we are in trouble because everyone is gone, and the sun is already behind the clouds," noted Tana.

Basil: "Somebody is in trouble, and it is oh so dark!"

Tana could hear in her head how she will get chewed out by her mom and dad who always told them to be in the house before the street lights come on. The sound of the howling wind and swirling leaves began to pick up in the air. The wind was churning the leaves in circles around the cold, dreary ground with great speed. Tana looked out among the many trees and watched the thick, dark trees move like they had a life of their own. Being outside caught in a terrible storm is what Tana hated the most. When Tana looked out at the edge of the park she saw there was not one person running home. Everyone was long gone. The trees were swaying even harder, as the wind picked up with a vengeance. Tana finally got her feet moving and started running towards the monkey bars. Jusssst as she caught up to Asa, she happened to see in the distance by the woods the squirrels running for dear life. Up the trees they scampered like someone was chasing them, but Tana could see why the wind was really starting to blow harder.

'Uhhh, who is that?' Tana wondered. 'Who is that standing there by those tall trees with that crazy looking outfit?'

Basil: "I know it ain't the ice cream man!"

CHAPTER 2

Tana could see it was a man hunched over just STANDING there, ever so still! He was leaning on a creepy looking zig zag cane. She noticed his hands covered the top of the cane. Tana noticed because his hands were BIG like baseball gloves, big! She thought to herself, 'my goodness gracious he was tall.' Tana also noticed as the trees whipped up around him, his long colorful coat blew open to reveal his crazy looking yellow pants. Looking down she saw he had long, wide, dark shoes. His shoes were so long they curled up at his toes. Tana thought how can a man walk with big feet, clown feet? 'Yeah,' she thought, 'clown feet.'

Basil: "Bababa boy those jokers are big! His shoes are so wide they look like dinner plates!"

When Tana looked up at his face it was blue. No, no she thought, his face was green. Slowly Tana clearly saw his dull looking face, and that is when it dawned on her he could be smiling at her. Ugh, she thought. He couldn't be looking at me! What made it even worse was Tana could clearly see there was one big, huge, gigantic, greasy looking, fat tooth hanging over his bottom lip.

'Yikes! That tooth was HUGE! It was soooo big it was the only tooth in his mouth. He could not fit another tooth in his mouth even if he wanted to,' thought Tana.

That is when Tana slowly realized he was looking straight at her, and that was all Tana needed to see. She quickly turned around and started to run for dear life, but she forgot her brother Asa. She figured she must be scared if she forgot her only brother. She spun back around looking throughout the park for Asa. For one quick second she thought she should leave him, because he made her so mad about hogging the bathroom. Of course she thought that was ridiculous to leave her brother behind, especially with a strange looking man in a weird looking coat. Tana started to panic, as she stared across the empty playground. As she scanned the park, she looked at all the park rides searching for Asa. Tana glanced at the shuffle board, no not there. She spun around again and saw the crooked playhouse, no not there either. Wait! There! Tana saw with relief. Asa was at the top of the new sliding board waving at her. Tana thought Asa looked like he did not have a care in the world. As Tana ran up to Asa, she started yelling at the top of her lungs.

"Asa! Come on!" shouted Tana.

Asa could tell something was wrong, because Tana's face always looked like a scared rabbit. Not that she looked like a rabbit, but boy those ears were big for a girl who was only seven years old. Asa immediately slid down the slide. Hmmm, wait a minute thought Asa. Did someone just push me, he thought? Once he got to the bottom of the slide he turned around and looked up at the top of the slide, but nobody was there. He forgot about that thought for the moment, because all he heard was Tana screaming and yelling at the top of her lungs. Asa could see Tana was heading for him at full speed. Since he thought about it he never saw Tana run so fast. Laughing to himself he thought she ran so fast her ears just about carried her off the ground. Now, Asa was scared. He did not want to look like a sissy, so he stood there laughing.

"You look like a scary cat Tana," Asa yelled.

As Tana ran up to her brother, she could not get the words out of her mouth fast enough because she was so frightened. She finally blurted out to her brother while gasping for air. As Tana stood there trying to get air back into her lungs gasping and heaving for breath, she pointed her finger at the edge of the park.

"Oh really, turn around. Do you see that hunched over man standing by the woods heading this way?" questioned Tana.

Asa turned to see the hunched over man with a zigzag cane. Asa saw how he was just standing there. Then he started walking towards them. As he began to approach them, his feet made a flip flopping sound because his feet were so big. He just kept staring at them smiling, as his face continued changing colors. Brother and sister noticed that icky smile with the big tooth which was really gross. The weird looking stranger beckoned with his finger for them to come to him. He was coming faster towards them like he was floating. Asa thought to himself, 'how did he do that?' Even though Asa was the older brother he was scared stiff. Though he was eight he was still scared of the boogeyman and any other thing that goes bump in the night. Asa started imagining all kinds of scary things. That's all he needed to see when he saw that creepy guy heading towards them. Asa grabbed Tana's hand and yelled for his sister to run.

"Come on, run!" exclaimed Asa.

They ran from the park. The clouds were darker than before and worst of all, the park was empty. Asa noticed the swings were swinging back and forth violently. 'Was someone pushing all the swings? Nah, it has to be the wind'. The leaves were swirling along the ground, and suddenly it felt cold. Asa never felt so scared even though Tana was with him. Little did Asa know that Tana was also scared. She was certain she heard a clicking sound like a tapping cane following behind them. The rain poured down, as they both turned the opposite way and started to run with the stranger behind them. The thundering and lightning made their feet run even faster, as they headed out of the park. Asa held onto his sister's hand. He was mad at her from this morning but realized he would do anything to protect her even from a scary looking man who was coming after them. Asa yelled at Tana above the noisy storm.

"Don't look back! Just keep running!"

Tana did not know why Asa said that because she had already released his hand and started running ahead of him. Tana could not run fast enough. She began to slow down when she could not hear the cane behind them, and Asa just about knocked her over trying to get away. Running out of breath she stopped and turned around. She thought no one was there but her and Asa. Asa was so busy running and yelling at her to run he did not realize the weird looking man was not there. Tana shouted at her brother to stop and look.

"Asa, stop! He's gone!"

When Asa finally slowed down he realize what Tana was saying when he turned around only to see the park in the distance. With the dark clouds eerily hovering over the playground they could both see the empty park. Bent over out of breath and breathing hard gasping for air Asa looked at Tana.

"Tana, what in the world was that? That man had yuck mouth, and what was up with those yellow pants?"

Just as hard as her brother, Tana was doubled over breathing with her hands on her knees.

"I don't know, but let's keep walking. I am not standing here so he can come get us," suggested Tana.

Asa was excited and scared. He started rambling on barely catching his breath, as they began walking.

"Tana, did you notice how sunny it is, and it stopped raining?"

"Yeah, but let's keep walking," said Tana.

The two continued talking about the strange looking man with the one tooth in his mouth and how everyone disappeared around them. What was even scarier was that they did not have a clue as to what was going on right underneath their noses at the park. They started heading downtown to Main Street, and continued looking over their shoulder every minute. 'That *man's tooth*' thought Asa '*was enough to give him nightmares for the next two weeks.*'

"Asa, you heard that cane clicking behind us?"

"Yeah!" Asa exclaimed.

"If we were running that fast, then how can a hunched over man with a zigzag cane and big clown feet run behind us? Or was he running after us?" Tana asked.

Basil: "Seriously?"

"I don't know Tana. I was just thinking the same thing."

Basil: "Seriously? You don't know either!"

"Let's go back home this way, it's quicker. We can cut through old man Harry's place," Tana ordered.

Even though old man Harry was mean none of the kids in the neighborhood were scared of him because he was just harmless old man Harry. Asa and Tana continued walking down the sidewalk on Main Street while old man Harry yelled from his window in the distance to stay off his lawn. Again Asa and Tana ignored old Harry and began going over the crazy events that just happened in the park. The both of them did not realize the streets were empty like a ghost town until they heard that dreaded clicking sound. Asa and Tana would not turn around, but they started running anyway.

"Asa, do you hear that?"

"Yeah! Don't turn around, just keep running!" Asa's heart was in his throat. The faster they ran the quicker the clicking sound came behind them. Asa was so scared he started crying while he was running. When he turned to look at Tana she was crying too. The thunder and lightning with the pouring rain made it even worse. As they cut through the backyard of another neighbor's house, thunder struck with a loud, ear splitting clap!

"Run Tana!" shouted Asa.

Basil: "As if you have to tell her twice."

Tana could not understand why Asa was yelling. She was ahead of him running like the wind. As they rounded the corner, they spotted their house. Tana had never been so happy to see her house which looked so safe. They reached the front door just about the same time knocking each other over. Asa forgot about being the big brother. He barely reached the door first turning the knob, BUT THE DOOR WAS LOCKED!

CHAPTER 3

Tana ran so fast she ran smack into her brother. By now they were both screaming and yelling, "mom, dad, open the door!"

The sound of the wind started howling, and the thunder made them both jump. When Tana turned, she saw Asa bawling like a newborn baby. Tana could not believe her big brother Asa was crying like a baby. Seeing her brother cry like that made her scream even louder. Suddenly the door swung open, and Tana and Asa fell into the foyer on the floor. They started screaming and babbling to their mom to 'shut the door.' As mom stood there with the door wide open, the scattered leaves flew through the house. Their mom immediately shut the door which took all her strength to keep out the storm's debris.

When she turned around she saw her two kids sitting on the floor crying and babbling nonstop like two scared chickens. Tana's hair was sticking straight out on her head like someone yelled 'boo' at her. Asa continued blubbering which their mom could not understand. As their mom stood there with her hands on her hips with an angry expression on her face, they realized their mom did not believe them. They tried telling their story again about the hunchback stranger in the park. Tana piped in how the stranger's face changed colors, and that's when mom had enough. The sound of their mom's reply to Tana and Asa made them realize their mom was angry.

"Really?" Mom asked. Mom had caught these two before with their wild stories only to find out it was all made up.

"Mom, we're not lying! He's out there!" Asa shouted.

Before they could even blink mom swung the door open to howling wind and pouring rain. When their mom saw nothing but an empty street she was really angry. That really did it. Mom scolded them for coming home late with their made up stories.

"You both know you are late coming home from the park so stop making up these wild stories. If I remember correctly you told me you were chased by an elephant the last time you were late. Do you know how worried I was?" Mom asked.

Tana and Asa knew they were doomed, especially when mom spoke in a low no nonsense tone. They knew all the lies they told before when they were late coming home just cost them their trust with mom ever believing them again.

"Now both of you get upstairs right now, and wash up for dinner! Your father and I will discuss your punishment after dinner."

As Asa and Tana trudged up the stairs, Asa looked at Tana with a questioning look on his face.

"You know what Tana? I didn't even believe it happened by the time we explained it. It sounds so whacky," Asa observed. Tana could only nod her head in agreement. As they went upstairs to the bathroom to wash their hands, they just looked at each other with hopelessness. Up the stairs they went thinking about how their mom did not believe them, and Tana being really mad and frustrated.

"We both saw that man!" Tana insisted.

"Of course we did you nit wit! You practically ran me over running home!"

"You're the one to talk! You were crying like a baby by the time we got home! You big baby! Wah,wah,wah, I am so scared!" mocked Tana.

Asa was so mad at his sister for making fun of him. He thought she was lucky he did not forget her running from the park. In the kitchen their mom heard them arguing. Hearing the back and forth bickering from downstairs their mom had enough of them. She came to the bottom of the stairs and yelled up to both of them.

"Both of you stop that fighting, and come downstairs for dinner! Now!" Mom beckoned. When mom said '*now*' they knew she was plenty mad. So they decided to stop fighting and come up with a plan after dinner. After washing up for dinner they headed downstairs hungry and tired. When Tana and Asa came into the kitchen their mom was already sitting at the table waiting with her foot tapping on the floor. '*Okay*' thought Asa, '*not a good sign.*' They also spotted dad at the head of the table. Hoping he would not see them, as they eased in their seats as quietly as possible waiting for the scolding. When dad looked from behind his newspaper he was not a happy camper. The look on his face was *not now, I'm hungry, and be quiet.* Asa and Tana knew they had a great dad and how he never gets mad. But boy their luck ran out that day.

"Okay, we have a wonderful dinner now let's say grace. Asa, please say grace, and we will talk about your day today and why you were both late," Mom stated with a stern look.

Basil: "Well, how nice. They look like the nice little family without a care in the world."

Mom launched into her day about what happened around the house, while Tana and Asa pretending they cared. Until...there was a rapid, loud knock at the door like a cane tapping sound. Asa and Tana practically jumped out of their seats from pure fright. Tana bolted under the table with Asa right behind her. Asa's eyes were big as saucers, as they hugged each other with fright. Both their mom and dad pulled the tablecloth back and told them to stop playing and to come out from under the table.

Asa slowly came back to his seat, but Tana wasn't moving. Dad got up to answer the door with mom right behind him. Now Tana and Asa could not see the door from the kitchen, but they could certainly hear their parents heading to the front door. After a few seconds Tana and Asa's curiosity got the best of them, so they inched behind the wall to see the front door. As they looked down the long hallway their dad reached for the doorknob, and the door suddenly swung open with a force. That was all Tana and Asa needed, and even though they did not see a thing they ran back under the table for cover. The tablecloth hid their view from whoever was at that door.

Suddenly the front door slammed shut. From under the table Asa looked at Tana and gulped. The quietness was deafening. Tana and Asa heard mom and dad's footsteps heading towards the kitchen. But there was no sound or screaming and no one talking at the door. Asa and Tana looked at each other and wondered what that was all about. Their parent's footsteps were slow, and their feet made a flapping sound, as they came down the hallway into the kitchen. Asa and Tana squeezed their eyes shut holding on to each other. That's when they heard their mother's voice.

"Tana and Asa you both better come out from under this table," Mom insisted.

Asa finally leaned over and lifted the tablecloth to look up at his mom standing there smiling. The problem was, when she smiled, she had one big, huge, gigantic, greasy, fat tooth at the top of her mouth! It was huge! It hung down over her bottom lip.

Basil: "Good foogly moo!"

Asa and Tana screamed. They scrambled from under the table running past their mom and dad and ran for their rooms. Their dad missed Tana running past him, but he just caught a hold of Asa's shirt. Not letting his father slow him down Asa shrugged and jerked away from his father's grip and ran for dear life. They could hear their mother coming up behind them on the stairs laughing, as she said in a weird, sing song voice.

"Okay you two, stop playing games," Mom said.

Tana could feel her mom right behind her, but she kept running. Asa ran in Tana's bedroom through the connecting bathroom rushing to lock the bedroom door. He jumped on Tana's bed and hid under the covers. Tana was right behind him slamming the door shut and locking it with trembling hands. Out of breath from running up the stairs or sheer fright she slid down to the floor looking at Asa yelling.

"What the heck was THAT following us?! This can't be real!" Tana yelled.

Tana realized she was talking to herself because Asa was still under the covers shaking like a leaf. The covers were even trembling. If Tana wasn't so scared she would have laughed at that sight. Then again, she thought his shaking under the covers made her mad, and that's when Tana yelled at Asa.

"ASA, answer me! Was that our mother?"

Peeking from under the blankets Asa could see Tana had a pleading look on her face, as her voice trembled on the edge of crying. Asa was not sure what was going on, and having his sister with that lost look on her face did not help matters.

"Ah, Tana, I don't know. I just saw mom with one ugly tooth in her mouth like that creepy guy at the park." As he came out from under the covers, he turned around to face his sister asking another terrifying question. "And what about dad?"

That's when Tana began rocking herself on the floor. She was thinking to herself, 'this cannot be real.' Then Asa broke into her thoughts.

"Tana, our mom has only one tooth in her mouth, and that man down there is not our dad!"

For a minute they sat there deep in thought about what just happened. Asa got off the bed and walked over to Tana. He may be a chicken, but he loved his sister. He was going to take care of her even though the creatures downstairs were not their mom and dad. Asa slid down the door to the floor next to Tana. He put his arm over her shoulders and told her it was going to be alright, although he didn't believe it himself. Looking at Tana really made Asa feel protective towards his sister, and he quietly whispered to her to keep her calm.

"You know what's really scary. When I ran up the stairs and turned around mom had a smile on her face with that one, big, fat tooth in her mouth," Asa whispered. Tana noticed it too, but she hoped it was her imagination.

Basil: "Not!"

"Tana, and..." Asa started.

Tana cut Asa off before he could finish. "No, I don't what to hear anymore!" Asa just kept talking on and on. She knew what he was going to say next and that set her teeth on edge. She saw it too.

"When I turned to look at mom I noticed those huge clown shoes on her feet, but I could not hear her going up the stairs. It's like she was floating up the stairs behind us," Asa said.

They looked at each other and wondered what to do next.

"We need to stop her from coming into our room," said Asa.

"HOW?" Tana asked.

What happened next made them break out in a sweat, as they sprung away from the door like someone bit them. It was their mom whispering to them on the other side of the door.

"I hear you two whispering. Now let's get ready for bed," Mom chuckled.

Was their mom standing by their door listening the entire time? It was like there was no door there because she sounded soooo close. Oh, so close. Asa and Tana jumped up from the floor and stood a distance away staring at Tana's door. As they backed away facing the door they were too scared to turn their backs for fear their mom might break through the door. The creepy sound of a clicking cane moving away from the other side of the door was getting quieter. Hearing that clicking sound of a cane going down the hallway Tana and Asa knew they were doomed. There was only one way out of their house and that was through the front door. After hearing the creepy cane Asa whispered with all the bravery he could muster.

"We need to stop her from coming into our room," Asa whispered.

Basil: "You think, Sherlock?"

"How?" Tana questioned.

"I don't know, but I will figure it out," Asa assured her.

"Where is dad?" asked Tana.

"Oh monkey buns! Tana I don't know!" Asa hollered.

Chapter 4

Tana realized Asa was really scared. He only said monkey buns when he was really scared and confused. Now that she thought about it, she was scared and really confused too. Her parents were creepy, and she felt there was no way out. She knew Asa would come up with a plan because he never gave up when they were in a fix. Well, except for the lie they told about the elephant chasing them home that time they were late. Now, Asa was deep into thought sitting on the bed. He was thinking the entire day did not make any sense, and where did the goofy guy with the zigzag cane disappear to? Was that him going down their hallway? He felt they were in danger, but he could not figure out what to do. He just needed a little time.

Basil: "Sure, take all the time in the world when your parents look like they are ready to eat you."

Asa and Tana were pooped from all the excitement, and now they were tired after eating a big dinner. So, with nothing else to do they got ready for bed. Asa even brushed his teeth. Now Tana knew he really was confused. Tana knew she needed to brush her teeth too. Her teeth felt furry, and she knew that she is supposed to brush after every meal. But she was too tired and she just couldn't focus. Deep in thought they both didn't have a choice about leaving. Where would they go? Once they were done getting ready for bed, they laid down on the floor looking up at the ceiling deep in thought. Until, there was a knock at the door, a persistent knocking. Asa and Tana jumped on Tana's bed watching the doorknob turn slowly back and forth. And all Tana and Asa could do was watch in fear. Tana quietly whispered to Asa.

"Good googly moo. Thank goodness I locked the door, or did I?"

They could hear the door trying to be pushed open, but the door was locked. Here's the surprise. Asa was choking with fear and could barely get the words out of his mouth.

"Who, who is it?" Asa stammered trying to get the words to come out.

"This is dad son, open the door. You sound scared. Are you and Tana okay?" Dad asked.

Both brother and sister sat up frozen still.

"Dad, is that you?" asked Asa.

"Of course. You know what? You two go to sleep and we will talk in the morning. Even though it'll be Saturday tomorrow I want you two up early. Do you both understand me?" asked Dad.

Tana and Asa were so numb with fear they nodded their heads 'yes.' But the strange thing was dad told them to stop nodding their heads, even though he could not see them on the other side of the door. Tana walked across the room and laid down on the floor. She turned over and started to quietly cry. Asa heard her crying, but he was just too scared to move. Then they fell asleep. Not only that, but they didn't come up with a plan. The birds were chirping, and the sun woke them up the next morning. Asa sat up like someone poked him. When he turned to look for Tana he sat up and yelled for her.

"What are you screaming for? I'm right here in the bathroom brushing my teeth," said Tana.

Basil: "Yes, he felt foolish."

"I thought you were gone or mom and dad snatched you. Sorry," Asa apologized with a tremor in his voice.

"That's okay. I know you were worried," Tana said.

If she said '*scared*' he would have denied it, and then they would start arguing. Well, after Asa finished dressing he sat on the bed next to Tana hoping to come up with something to make her feel better.

While sitting on the bed with the silence between them Asa came up with an idea.

"Let's sneak out of here quick."

"What about mom and dad?" Tana observed.

"First of all, that ain't mom and dad."

"Asa there is no such word as ain't. The word is 'isn't'."

Basil: "Oh that's just great, now we have time for English lessons when your parents are downstairs with a tooth in their mouth!"

"Whatever, Tana. Anyway, they probably think we are still asleep so now is the time to sneak out of here before they realize what's going on. Tana, go and look out the door."

Tana looked at her brother, as if he lost his mind. "No! You're the older brother you open the door!"

They finally decided after much arguing they would do it together. Walking over to the door made Asa's heart race. He was too scared to even put his hand on the doorknob. After much talking to himself Asa eased the bedroom door open and found it very quiet in the hallway. It was still, very still. They peeked out and looked both ways down the hallway. Not a sound came from their parents bedroom or downstairs. Slowly Tana and Asa eased along the wall of the hallway toward the stairs. Tana started to giggle and could not stop. Tana could not for the life of her figure out why she started to laugh. Asa put a stop to it quickly. Asa spun around hissing in a whispered voice.

"Be quiet! What is so funny Tana?"

Tana knew it was stupid, but she could not help herself. She looked at her brother and whispered to him with the giggles still in her throat, "I can't help it!"

"Well, you better stop or we will be staring at our one tooth mom!"

Basil: "That pretty much shut her up."

As they continued down the hall, the clock on the wall struck 9:00AM. Tana and Asa stood along the wall frozen with fear. This made them move faster to the top of the staircase. When they reached the staircase they knew there was that one step that always creaked.

This meant only one thing and that was to jump over it and keep running. Suddenly there was a loud crash that came from the kitchen. Quickly Asa looked at Tana and whispered "one two, three." They leaped over the creaky step at the same time.

Tana fell all the way down the stairs behind Asa, and Asa barely held the railing. They had managed to reach the bottom of the stairs at the same time. When they made it to the door Asa turned the knob, but it was locked. As much as Asa attempted to turn the doorknob with Tana breathing down his neck, he wondered why the door was locked. As soon as Asa's last thought ran through his mind there was a loud crash in the kitchen again. Asa continued to struggle turning the doorknob, but his hands kept slipping and sliding around the knob. Asa was so scared he did not realize his hands were sweaty. Tana kept nudging him to hurry, but he just could not open the door. Finally, Tana pushed her brother out of the way and tried to open the door herself. Her hands started to slip too but couldn't turn the knob because of Asa's yucky, slippery hands. That is when they heard their mom-if that was really their mom. 'Oh, there goes that creepy sing song voice again' thought Asa.

"Tana and Asa are you up?" Mom asked.

Basil: "Yep. It's them alright!"

Tana and Asa looked over their shoulder towards the kitchen only to see a huge pair of clown shoes coming around the corner. 'That's it' thought Asa, whoever that woman was she was not going to catch him. Tana and Asa turned back towards the door. They knocked each other out of the way furiously attempting to open the door. Tana knocked her brother out of the way again and used her shirt to open the door. Finally the door swung open. Once Tana opened the door they bolted out of there like their pants were on fire. They kept running down the block until they got around the corner. After running a couple of blocks they finally stopped to catch their breath. Looking down the block they could not see anyone chasing them. As the sister and brother tried holding each other up from the long run down the street, each kept a sharp lookout for their creepy looking parents. Frighten and gasping for breath Tana yelled at her brother even though he was standing next to her.

"'Did you see those crazy clown shoes coming around the corner?'"Tana exclaimed.

"Yeah, and I am not going back there!" Asa insisted.

"Then, what are we going to do?"

"I don't know Tana." Asa replied.

While catching their breath they saw Scooter and Pumpkin coming up the block.

"That's just great, now we have another problem. The last people we need to see are Pumpkin and Scooter," Tana said angrily.

Pumpkin wasn't so bad. It was that bully Scooter that all the kids hated. Scooter just loved making fun of anyone no matter what they look like, especially if it was a girl. He always had a smirk on his face even when he was by himself. Tana thought the freckles on his face were the only thing that made him cute. Tana noticed Scooter was leaning towards pudgy, as he walked down the sidewalk. '*Maybe that's why he is always mad, but that was it as far as cuteness,*' thought Tana.

Tana knew Scooter was a terror to the kids at school and to the teachers too. No one wanted to talk to him because he never had anything nice to say. He always hung out with the crowd that constantly bothered other kids. It was like they had nothing else to do but make people miserable. Tana knew it was because he had low self-esteem, and also he was always angry. That is why he had only one friend which was Pumpkin. No one knew why Pumpkin was friends with him because Pumpkin was a nice kid. He was tall, slim, and easy going. He loved wearing sneakers and jeans and always had a smile on his face. One thing Pumpkin always did was mumble. Mumble here mumble there. Folks always asked him to repeat himself. One couldn't help loving Pumpkin. Asa and Tana dreaded their meeting with Scooter, but it was too late to run because Scooter already spotted them from down the block. They figured if they ran he would chase them down. While standing there Asa had an idea. He looked at Tana and whispered to her to follow his lead just before Pumpkin and Scooter came within earshot.

"What are you two lame brains doing on the sidewalk?" Scooter sneered.

"Oh, Tana and I were running because we thought we saw something strange in the park," replied Asa. Scooter already started with a sneer on his face.

"You two sissy nissys," Scooter mocked.

Scooter was tall and oogly because he was not nice. When you're mean toward other people then you are just plain oogly. It's even worse than ugly. Tana caught on to what Asa was doing so she joined in.

"Well, I don't know Scooter. We were really scared," said Tana.

Tana knew a bully always had a lot of bravado, but underneath they were too scared to admit to any kind of feelings. And Pumpkin, he just stood there. But he was smart enough to know when anything scary was going on he did not want any part of it. One could see he was ready to turn and bolt down the sidewalk the other way. Without taking his eyes off Asa and Tana, Scooter held on to Pumpkin by the shirt before he could spin around and run. Scooter threatened Pumpkin he better not move.

"Yeah right! I'm scerrrd! You two little sissy nissys scared little babies. Let's go. I want to see what you two lame brains are so scared of," Scooter said.

Scooter thought he was the king of the neighborhood, but all the kids thought he was the big head bully of the neighborhood. Tana and Asa did not care what Scooter thought, and they were not stupid. They were smart enough to walk at least ten steps behind Scooter and Pumpkin just in case the hunchback stranger was there. They also remembered very clearly how fast this weird looking guy moved. They wanted a head start run just in case. When they arrived at the park it was a nice day, and there were a few kids hanging around by the slide and merry go round. Scooter turned and looked at Asa and Tana and began to tease them.

"Oh yeah, I'm so scared," mocked Scooter.

Tana wanted to whack him to the ground, but she was busy watching what was in those trees at the edge of the park. Asa was practically standing on her back because he was shaking so bad in his weird looking sneakers. Scooter was bored with them by now seeing there was nothing out there to scare him. This was fine with Asa, as Scooter and Pumpkin turned and walked the other way toward the rides. Asa and Tana could see Scooter started pushing kids off the swings, and Pumpkin was on the sliding board smiling of course at all the girls. So, that left Tana and Asa standing there in the middle of the park waiting for something to happen.

Basil: "Well, nothing happened, yet!"

Tana could not believe how long they were at the park, and nothing popped out of the trees. After a while Tana and Asa started to relax and enjoy the park since they were so wound up from their crazy experience at home. They knew they needed to do something about mom and dad, but it was too much to think about. All their friends were there anyway. It was just a beautiful day at the park.

Basil: "NOT."

After spending all day at the park Asa walked over to Tana with a look of worry. Slowly Tana began to realize why they had to go home. The sun was setting over the park, and the kids started heading for home.

Basil: "Oh boy, here we go again."

Even though it was summertime the clouds started setting in. The swings started moving like they had a life of their own. Tana and Asa just looked at each other. Pumpkin was at the top of the slide. He was so busy looking down at the ground talking to a girl he did not realize what was going on around him. Scooter was on the merry go round happy that he bullied all the kids off of it while he went around in circles.

Basil: "Scooter is oogly!"

While Tana and Asa were standing by the monkey bars trying to decide where to run to, it all started again. Suddenly Pumpkin fell all the way down the slide head first, like he was pushed. 'Goodness gracious' thought Tana, it was like someone pushed him. Pumpkin jumped up, as soon as he hit the ground. He immediately stood up and looked at the top of the slide to see who pushed him. But, no one was there. He just knew someone pushed him, BUT NO ONE WAS THERE!

No sooner than Pumpkin figured it out, he happened to glance out of the corner of his eye. He spotted something strange at the edge of the park, with yellow pants? Meanwhile, the merry go round started to spin a little faster with Scooter on it. Tana wondered how was that merry go round spinning so fast? Yep, Scooter began having second thoughts about what Tana and Asa said. He saw the stranger at the edge of the woods, once the merry go round started to slow down. Asa watched what happened to Scooter and gulped. One has to ask, why did Asa gulp? The merry go round was spinning much slower, and Scooter was not on it. Pumpkin witnessed all of this, and that was all he needed.

Tana and Asa turned to see Pumpkin running from the park. All they saw was the back of his sneakers. Boy he was fast! The poor girl he left by the slide was just dumbfounded. She did not understand what was going on. So she just turned around embarrassed and headed for home disappointed that Pumpkin left her standing there.

Basil: "You talk about clueless!"

Meanwhile, Tana and Asa were staring at the slowly spinning merry go round.

"Oh great. Juuusst great! Tana, where is Scooter? I don't even like the guy, but where is he Tana?" Asa whined.

"I don't know!" Tana responded

"I know," said the Stranger.

Asa felt this strong, cold wind blowing down his back which made him jump. He spun around only to be facing the man with the big fat greasy tooth and clown shoes. This time his face was yellow like his pants, no, no, now his face started turning blue thought Asa. He knew

Tana was next to him because she started moaning. Asa screamed. He was so terrified he took off screaming leaving Tana behind. Running down the block realizing what he just did, he turned around to go back for her. Once he ran back all he saw was an empty park that was raining with lightning, thunder, and no Tana. Until he felt a hand on his shoulder, Asa was so frightened he let out a yelp. It was Tana.

CHAPTER 5

When Asa realized it was his sister he screamed at her at the top of his lungs.

"Oh Monkey Buns! Don't you ever do that again!" Asa yelled.

"Don't you ever leave me like that again!! You're lucky I took off running first! I was going to get help!" Tana replied feeling guilty.

"What? Yeah right!" yelled Asa.

"Look, let's go! Why are we standing here arguing?. "

Asa shook his head "We gotta find Scooter!"

"Asa, there is no such word as gotta."

Ignoring his sister's correction Asa gave up finding Scooter again.

"You go right ahead, because I am out of here!" Tana exclaimed.

Well, you didn't have to tell Asa twice because he was right behind Tana with Scooter long forgotten. As they were running like sprinters from the park, they constantly turned looking over their shoulders expecting to hear that clicking sound with yellow pants chasing them. What they did see from a distance was the park had the dark clouds hovering over it, and it was pouring rain just over the park. But the rest of the neighborhood was completely sunny. Even the birds were singing.

Asa and Tana knew they had nowhere to go. Both of them had no idea what would be waiting for them at home, and they did not have the stomach to see another big greasy tooth on an empty stomach. So, they stood on the sidewalk in the middle of downtown Seward on a bright sunny day. Even though Seward was a small town it usually had a few people out and about. Looking up and down the sidewalk Tana could see the town was practically empty. Looking at each other on a warm sunny day made Asa cold with fear.

"Come on Tana, let's go inside the ice cream shop across the street."

"Yeah, that sounds like a good idea," Tana replied.

While crossing the street the wind started to pick up, and the dark clouds appeared to be hovering close by in the distance. They made their way across the street, as it started to rain. Once inside Tana and Asa noticed how packed it was with people. There were huge banners throughout the shop about the strawberry festival being held in town.

"I forgot there was the strawberry festival today," recalled Tana.

Since Tana and Asa could not find a seat they stood by the large window plotting their next move. Asa was getting hungry and ice cream was not the food he wanted. Plus, neither one of them had any money. His parents believed kids were supposed to help around the house without getting paid to do it.

"I'm hungry and we don't have any money," Tana noted.

"Let me think Tana," said Asa.

Asa could see his sister was ready to fall apart, and he could not blame her. Heck, he was scared. Asa looked at Tana to reassure her that things were okay until something caught his attention outside across the street. Asa was convinced he saw someone stooping behind a parked car. What was bothersome about it was the figure had on a long colorful coat. The problem: It was 83 degrees. You know that gut feeling you get when your stomach flops, and your hair stands on the back of your neck? Well, that is what Asa was feeling.

Tana watched him closely, and followed his eyes across the street. She did not see anything at first. But wait, 'what was that person doing behind that car,' thought Tana? Only then did she clearly see what Asa was looking at. The clown shoes! Those big, horrendous looking clown shoes staring at them. She could see the long coat peeking out from behind the car. But she could not see his face. Tana reached for Asa's arm without taking her eyes off whoever was behind the car across the street. Slowly the one huge shoe slowly inched its way from behind the car. It was like the shoe knew it was being watched. Before they could scream the man's face darted out from behind the car, like a jack in the box. It was him! Oh that, big gruesome looking tooth was staring right at them! His arm reached out and beckoned them to come to him. Now that was scary.

Asa and Tana ran without hesitation towards the back of the ice cream shop ducking all the people. When they made it to the back of the shop they heard the door chimes of the shop ring out, but it was strangely quiet. Tana and Asa did not hear a pin drop from all the people in the front of the shop. But they sure heard the clicking sound of a cane coming closer. This time Asa had Tana's hand, and he spotted the back door. They heard someone yelling behind them, "They cannot run through the shop." That was no problem for Tana and Asa. Once they ran through the kitchen and out the back door Asa noticed there was no clicking sound following them. 'Whew, what a relief' he thought. Asa and Tana kept running for their lives. When they ran a few blocks they finally slowed down to catch their breath. Asa was panting like a runaway train, and Tana was breathing just as hard.

"Tana, I think this weirdo is trying to catch us, but I don't know why," wheezed Asa. Tana could barely get out the one word.

"Duh! I thought the same thing! It seems like he could snatch us off the street, but he cannot catch us."

"I thought it was weird that we could not hear all those people in the ice cream shop when we were in the back of the kitchen."

"Yeah! Just like when mom and dad answered the door. Remember when it went quiet for a few seconds! What is that all about?"

Neither one of them could come up with any answers, as they were walking around in circles through the neighborhood. Not only were they desperate to find somewhere to hide, but they could not go home until they could figure out who were the two creepy people in their house. Walking through the neighborhood Asa was driving Tana nuts with his endless questions. So she was glad when she spotted the house at the end of town. Pointing down the street Tana suddenly had hope.

"Asa look! There's Pumpkin's house!"

They knew Pumpkin had to be home because he took off from the park like his pants were on fire. As they ran up to Pumpkin's door the wind began to blow with the leaves swirling around the yard. Pumpkin had a lot of trees in his front yard, and the shrubs were really tall bordering along the sidewalk. You couldn't see the sidewalk for the tallness of the shrubs in his yard. Asa and Tana were getting nervous because the weather was turning again. Every time the weather turned for the worse, well they did not want to think about it.

Asa and Tana kept knocking praying someone would open that door. Then it started. That dreaded clicking sound. Their observation of the weather made them bang on the door even louder and faster. They were trapped! You could not reach Pumpkin's backyard seeing there was a gate there for his dog Butch. Pumpkin's dog Butch is a Chihuahua. So they knew they were in trouble because Butch would not be of any help. The rain began to come down really hard, and the clicking was getting louder. Asa turned around in time to see the one big, fat shoe coming around the shrub. Asa started screaming for someone to open the door. Low and behold that's when Pumpkin finally opened the door. As Pumpkin opened the door looking past his friends, Tana and Asa could see his face which looked like he saw a ghost. Pumpkin's eyes were huge. Seeing his frightened face Asa and Tana ran straight past Pumpkin falling onto the floor. Pumpkin slammed the door so fast he nearly closed it on them.

"Hey, you nearly chopped us in half with the door!" shouted Asa.

"That's because I just saw a man with yellow pants and a green face floating towards us!" Pumpkin yelled while locking the door.

Basil: "Yikes! Well folks, what do you think happened next? Yep, there was a knock at the door!"

All three of them stood frozen looking at the door like three stone statues. They jumped out of their skin yelling when the voice behind them spoke.

"Are you three going to stand there or is someone going to open the door? What is going on with you kids, and why on earth are you screaming?" asked Mr. Smith.

As Mr. Smith headed for the door walking past them all three kids yelled in unison, "Don't open the door!" But of course he did in one fell swoop. And what did Mr. Smith see? He saw nothing but the wind howling and the rain pouring down. Asa, Tana, and Pumpkin looked at each other like they just saw another ghost. Mr. Smith stood there looking at his son and his two little friends with great curiosity. Mr. Smith figured it was just the wind.

"Elliot, are you going to tell me what's going on?" demanded Mr. Smith.

Tana and Asa did not know what Pumpkin's real name was. Only his parents called him Elliot. Now Pumpkin knew if he told his dad what he saw at the park and what he thought was heading up their front steps, his dad would not believe him. Pumpkin thought about the last time he told a whopper of a story, and his dad grounded him so fast his head was spinning for days with boredom. So he just said they were playing a game, and they got too loud. So Mr. Smith told them to go upstairs if they wanted to play. Pumpkin liked that idea anyway so they could get away from the door. Before they ran upstairs, Pumpkin's dad invited Asa and Tana for dinner which they readily agreed as he shut and locked his door.

"Make sure you call your parents to let them know where you are," advised Mr. Smith.

Basil: "HA! Is he kidding?"

Asa hesitated, but he told Mr. Smith he would call home, only he had to go to the bathroom first. They all ran upstairs, and Pumpkin slammed the door and locked it. You would have thought the man with the yellow pants was right there behind him. Tana scrambled to the floor, and Asa stood by the window looking out at the dark night. Pumpkin remained standing because his room was such a mess there was nowhere to sit.

"Sheesh! This room is a mess, don't you ever clean it?" asked Tana.

"You can clean it for me," replied Pumpkin.

Pumpkin shoved his clothes off the chair and sat at his computer. Pumpkin's hands were shaking like a leaf, and his eyes were constantly darting back and forth across the room. He was making Tana and Asa more nervous with his crazy antics.

"Why do I feel like you guys know what's going on? That thing in the park was creepy, and I know I will have nightmares for the rest of my life! Now that creature showed up at my door thanks to you two!" accused Pumpkin.

"Wait a cotton picking minute. You did not have to go to the park! We didn't make you come! You and Scooter didn't believe us so you came," added Tana.

Hearing Tana's blabby voice made Pumpkin start thinking of the crazy day. He would do anything to stop her from talking, but it was too late. 'Boy she was chatty, thank goodness all girls were not like this' thought Pumpkin. Now he could see why Scooter did not like them. The more he thought about it Scooter did not like anyone. '*Wait a minute*', thought Pumpkin, '*where is his friend Scooter?*'

"Hey! Where's Scooter?" asked Pumpkin.

There was a silence in the room. No one spoke, and all you heard was the ticking of Pumpkin's clock on the wall.

"You saw what happened. Why are you asking us? We don't know what happened to Scooter either," said Asa.

"Ah man, are you kidding me? You mean Scooter just disappeared into thin air? Are you serious?" Pumpkin asked incredulously.

"Why don't we call his house and see if he's there," Tana suggested.

"Yeah, that's a good idea!" Asa replied.

"Okay, let's go," said Pumpkin.

Pumpkin unlocked his door and ran downstairs to the hall phone with Asa and Tana trailing behind him. He picked up the phone and began to dial. Leaning over Pumpkin's shoulder Asa and Tana heard the voice on the other end of the phone, but they could not make out the words. Asa could not hear the conversation, but he realized the way Pumpkin answered Scooter was home. Pumpkin hung up the phone and turned around looking a little relieved.

"What happened?" Asa inquired.

"His mom said Scooter is home," Pumpkin replied.

"Scooter's home?" asked Tana.

"Yeah, and she told me he just got home and went straight to bed," Pumpkin answered.

"But its pitch black out there, and he just got home?" Asa observed.

"Yeah," Pumpkin agreed.

Pumpkin's Dad came around the corner and opened the door, and told the kids that dinner was ready and to wash up. He asked Asa if he called his parents. Asa couldn't lie so he knew he had to make that dreaded call. Tana stepped back three steps to the wall.

Basil: "Like she's going somewhere!"

Asa walked slowly to the phone like it was ready to hit him in the head. As Tana and Pumpkin stood there they could hear the wind continue to howl with the rain pouring down outside. With the phone to his ear Asa waited nervously for someone to answer the phone. The only problem was the sound of the repeating clicking was just a loud ....click, click, click. Asa slowly put the phone down and tried to calm himself.

CHAPTER 6

"What is it? Asa what is it?" Tana pleaded.

After he told Pumpkin and Tana what happened he decided they were not going home. Asa just realized Mr. Smith made his plan a little easier. Mr. Smith thought Asa called his parents so he told them they could stay over seeing that it was late, and the weather was really bad. Asa found Mr. Smith in the kitchen, and told Pumpkin's father he called and asked his parents if he and Tana could stay over, and he lied even further. He told Mr. Smith his parents thanked him, and said they could spend the night.

"No problem Asa. Okay guys, mom and I are waiting for you. Let's eat!" Mr. Smith answered.

Asa breathed a sigh of relief. He did not get any more questions from Mr. Smith. Coming up with spending the night was a last minute idea Asa came up with. Once his lies were done his stomach began to growl from hunger.

Basil: "His pants should be toasty and burnt from all that lying."

All three kids sat down trying to hold on to their sanity which was really becoming hard to do, until the food was passed around the table. Tana, Asa, and Pumpkin put up with Mr. and Mrs. Smith's questions about school. Tana was very polite but on edge. So Asa took over the conversation giving a good performance that nothing was wrong. After dinner was done everyone was so relaxed they waited gleefully for dessert to be served. Even Pumpkin forgot their problems for the moment when there was a knock on the door. Tana and Asa dove under the table, and not knowing where else to hide as Pumpkin followed them. Because he knew THEY KNEW what was going to happen next. Mr. and Mrs. Smith were surprised with their behavior, and told all of them to come out from under the table.

Basil: "Does this sound familiar?"

"Is someone going to answer the door?" asked Pumpkin.

"When all of you come out from under there I will answer it. Elliot you know better than to play around during dinner. What is wrong with you?" Mr. Smith questioned.

The three of them slowly returned to their seats, as they waited and watched for a gross tooth to bust through the door. Pumpkin was turned half way out of his seat facing the kitchen door. Pumpkin always believed in getting a good head start. Tana felt the same way because she was not going to be caught by a one tooth monster. Dad went to the door with Pumpkin's mom right behind him. Pumpkin, Tana, and Asa were frozen in their chairs until there was this sudden booming voice coming from the hallway.

"How long were you two going to leave me out there?" questioned Uncle Marcus.

Pumpkin immediately recognized his uncle's voice. He tore out of his seat and ran to hug his Uncle Marcus. You see, Uncle Marcus was a computer nerd with the big thick glasses and an easy laugh. Uncle Marcus was tall and slim like Pumpkin, but his uncle could not see worth a lick without his glasses. Even though his uncle was twenty-two years old he always took time out for Pumpkin. He took Pumpkin everywhere with him even though his schedule with his job was always busy. Since he moved to the West coast Pumpkin's family did not see him as much. Mr. and Mrs. Smith were excited to have Uncle Marcus come and visit after being away for a long period of time. With plenty of hugging, introductions, and laughing everyone settled back down to the dinner table.

Basil: "Now isn't this great. Everyone is sitting down at the table having dessert, and asking questions about Uncle Marcus being in town. But the night is not over! He, he, he. "

"So, when did you get in town? Why didn't you call us?" Mr. Smith asked.

"I didn't want you guys to go to any trouble, plus I have a rental car outside. I am here in Seward on a job with the phone company. They needed someone to come out here and make sure the office staff got enough help. We have been having problems with the phone lines in this little town, and this was the perfect time for me to come visit my family. So, how is my favorite sister?" Uncle Marcus inquired.

Uncle Marcus loved his sister. That's because she could not see two feet in front of her. Her glasses were thicker than his! So there was a special bond between the two mostly because they were teased in school by all the kids. Pumpkin's mom Michelle was only a few years older than her brother, but she was always thankful that he always looked after her son. That was good enough for her.

"Marcus, how long will you be staying?" asked Mr. Smith.

"As long as it takes me to find out what is going on with this phone system. It could be days or weeks."

"Where are your bags? Aren't you staying with us?" asked Pumpkin.

"Of course, I just have too many bags to tote to the house."

"Well, let Elliot and Gene grab your bags. Marcus, why don't you sit down and eat. You must be starving," Mom replied.

Asa, Tana, and Pumpkin looked at each other across the table trying to figure out who would be brave enough to go out there and get the bags. Asa was the first to get up from the table. He realized he just couldn't sit there twiddling his thumbs. He looked across the table at Pumpkin who was looking at his Uncle Marcus like he was interested in the conversation. Asa knew Pumpkin was scared because he refused to look his way. Knowing not how to delay getting the bags Asa finally headed for the door. Mr. Smith had to nudge Pumpkin out of his seat scolding him for letting his friends do all the work. Trailing slowly behind Asa, Pumpkin walked behind Tana trying to figure out how not to go outside. Asa put his hand on the doorknob, but he would not open the door. All three of them stood there staring at each other silently wishing they were somewhere else.

Basil: "Ah go on, someone open the door, and see what's on the other side."

The kids could hear the adults in the kitchen talking and chatting away. All Pumpkin heard from the doorway was his Uncle Marcus stating he would get the bags.

"No, I ate in town. The dessert looks great. That will be good enough for me. Gene, let me help those guys get my bags," Uncle Marcus replied coming down the hallway.

Pumpkin waited, as his father and Uncle Marcus went past them to open the door. Asa and Tana stood there as well. Pumpkin was not helping anyone with that scared look on his face. One little 'boo' and he would be gone. Mr. Smith reached for the doorknob while Tana and Asa stood back holding their breath. The door flew open knocking Mr. Smith and Uncle Marcus backwards a few steps. The wind howled with the trees blowing back and forth in the dark night, as the rain continued to pour.

"Wow, this is weird. The rest of the town was sunny today, and now it's absolutely dark out here," Uncle Marcus observed.

"This is strange. I thought it was going to be sunny. Oh well, let's get these bags," Mr. Smith answered.

"I keep forgetting how dark it is out here at the edge of town," Uncle Marcus noted.

Basil: "Oh yeah, darker than the bottom of a clown's shoe!"

Living on the edge of town did not help either because the street lights stopped a block before Pumpkins house. The three of them stood by the door like statues imagining all kinds of scary things. Pumpkin's dad stood there for a brief moment looking up at the sky wondering what was going on with the weather. Uncle Marcus and Mr. Smith headed down the sidewalk with Mr. Smith yelling over his shoulder.

"Are you and Asa going to stand by the door and stare, or help us with the bags?" Dad asked.

Basil: "I bet a monkey's uncle they will stand by that door and stare and run up the stairs if anything moved with big shoes."

"No worries, those bags are too heavy for them anyway. Let me help you," Uncle Marcus insisted.

Tana held the door waiting for them to come back with Asa standing behind her.

"Sure is dark out there," said Tana.

"Yeah, but we have to guard the door and slam it shut just in case. Right, Pumpkin... Pumpkin?" said Asa.

When Asa and Tana turned they found an empty spot behind them. Pumpkin was gone!

"Where did he go?" Asa asked.

"I don't know, he was just standing here a second ago," Tana said.

When Tana turned, she found Pumpkin at the top of the stairs.

"Psst, I'm up here. I just wanted to make sure my room door was open just in case we would have to run upstairs," Pumpkin explained.

"You knuckle head! Come back down here!" Asa yelled.

Mr. Smith came through the doorway with some of the bags setting them on the floor in the hallway.

"That's okay Asa, we have all the bags. Why don't you two go on upstairs and talk to Pumpkin," Mr. Smith said.

"Yes sir," Asa assented.

As Asa closed the door the wind started to blow mighty fierce, and it was a cold wind stirring up those leaves. Asa slammed the door shut and locking it not wanting to see anything come out of the dark. Tana and Asa realized they had a problem: They could not go home as long as their parents were acting weird, and especially mom with one tooth in her mouth, and floating. Not knowing what to do Tana and Asa walked up the stairs while trying to come up with a plan. Once they were in Pumpkins room Asa closed the door shut and locked it. He took to locking doors lately. Lying on top of the pile of clothes, Pumpkin laid staring up at the ceiling with a dazed look on his face. Watching Pumpkin, Tana thought to herself, 'there he goes again with that mumbling and babbling under his breath.'

"What is wrong with you Pumpkin?" asked Asa.

"What is wrong?!! Are you kidding! There is an ugly looking man chasing us with yellow pants, with a gross fat tooth, Scooter disappears from the park only to show up at home in the middle of the night, and you two can't go home!!!" Pumpkin exclaimed.

Basil: "I bet they heard him this time!"

"Oh I get it, you're scared thinking that weirdo man might come here, and it's our fault!" Tana said.

"Du-uuh! Heck yeah I'm scared, aren't you?!! What are you guys going to do?" Pumpkin squeaked.

"You mean what are WE going to do?" Asa corrected.

"Guys, we might as well stop fighting, because this is not getting us anywhere! Pumpkin, we don't even have a home to go to. At least you have a roof over your head, and your parents have teeth in their mouth! Once tomorrow comes Asa and I have to figure out what to do," Tana responded.

Basil: "Boy, wasn't that fun? They are so busy fighting no one is looking out that window. Ohhh guys...."

But they do notice the windows rattle, and the wind noise picks up. Pumpkin hears it, and dives under the pile of clothes on his bed wishing again he was somewhere else. Asa looked at Pumpkin and shook his head as he headed towards the window.

"Sheesh! It's only the wind Pumpkin," Asa explained. Asa goes to lock the window, and looks out at the trees, but he froze when he looked out into the backyard. Pointing with a shaky finger he quietly mumbles under his breath. "Oh no. That creepy guy is sitting in the tree over there."

"What did you say?" asked Tana.

Asa was frozen in his shoes, and no matter how he tried he could not move his feet to turn and run. All he could do was point to the window towards the trees in Pumpkin's backyard.

"Look Tana," Asa trembled with a shaky voice.

Tana could not understand why her brother was mumbling under his breath, and why was he pointing at the window. Tired and frustrated Tana walks over to the window. Sitting in the tree is the man with the crooked cane and the big fat greasy looking tooth staring directly at them. Now brother and sister were frozen in their shoes looking at this weird man, and him staring back. He just kept looking at them with an empty look on his face. What shook them out of their daze was their buddy Pumpkin screaming at the top of his lungs.

"Asa! Close the curtains!" bellowed Pumpkin.

Asa finally leaped into action and slammed the curtains shut. He was breathing so hard even old man Harry could probably hear his heart beating down the street. Tana started backing up.

Basil: "Yeah right! Like she has somewhere to go!"

Asa finally unglued himself from the floor and turned to see his sister backing up.

"Tana, where are you going?"

"We have to tell Pumpkin's parents! We can't do this by ourselves!! We are only kids!!! Right, Pumpkin?"

She turned to look at Pumpkin shaking under the mountain of clothes.

Basil: "I think Pumpkin has had enough. Don't you?"

Coming from underneath the mound of clothes he shakily agreed with Tana.

"We gotta tell my parents guys. We got a crazy man sitting in the tree in the backyard with a crooked cane!" added Pumpkin.

Asa could obviously see Pumpkin was ready to run through the door if he did not stop him.

"If we go downstairs and tell your parents, you know what will happen if they go out there to look. That thing out there could grab them, then what?" asked Asa.

Basil: "What, what now?"

"Forget my parents, let's call the police, and then we tell my parents! At least they have guns!" suggested Pumpkin. After Pumpkin's heart slowed down a bit his curiosity got the better of him. "Is it still out there?"

"How would I know!" Asa retorted.

"Tana go check and see," Pumpkin said.

"I can't believe how chicken you are!" accused Tana.

"I don't see you running over there ripping open the curtains! At least I told you to close them!" Pumpkin replied.

"Shut up you guys! I'll go look! Pumpkin, turn out the light so he won't be able see us. Tana stoop down, because I will peek through the curtains," Asa whispered.

Basil: "Now the room was blacker than the bottom of a worn out clown shoe!"

Pumpkin stayed by the door just in case he needed to run. He thought every man for himself if that thing got in his room. He wanted to run, but he was too scared to move. He wanted to cry, but Tana was there, and he didn't want to cry in front of a girl. But he was awfully close.

"Tana, are you okay?" Asa asked.

"Yes," whispered Tana.

"Pumpkin, where are you?" asked Asa.

"Where do you think, by the door!" Pumpkin hissed.

Shaking his head Asa whispers to himself, "Figures."

It was a big window, so Asa went to the middle of the window to open the curtains. Then he thought better of it, and went to the end of the window. Asa eased to the side of the window, and he just took a pieeece of the curtain. He also took some deep breaths before he eased that curtain open, because his hands were shaking. Just an inch, because that man sitting in that tree was just, what?

Basil: "How should one say it?.....scary?"

When Asa opened the curtain the Stranger's face was right there staring right back at him inches from the window pane, up close and personal. The curtain fell back with Asa letting out a scream, and he fell backwards trying to turn and run. He didn't realize that was Tana he tripped over. Just before Asa opened the curtain Tana had decided to move behind him on the floor to peek over his shoulder. Pumpkin started screaming, because Asa was screaming. Pumpkin didn't see a thing, but that screaming from Asa was enough for him. He unbolted the door and ran downstairs to his parents in the living room.

Basil: "Did I tell you he was screaming too?"

Pumpkin took those stairs two at a time running. He was screaming with gibberish noises coming out of his mouth all the way down the stairs. Pumpkin's parents and his Uncle Marcus were sitting in the living room startled when Pumpkin came in the room blabbing away. All the adults jumped out of their seats seeing Pumpkin running into the room screaming like he was being attacked.

"Elliot what in the world is going on? Calm down! What is wrong?" asked Mr. Smith.

"The, the, the room! The room! Upstairs!" Pumpkin stuttered.

All the grownups ran for the stairs thinking something was wrong with Tana and Asa. Of course Pumpkin was close behind them. He wasn't staying in any room by himself. As Mr. Smith ran in the room with Mrs. Smith and Uncle Marcus close behind him, he found Tana and Asa sitting on the bed calmly laughing.

Basil: "Okay, these two are creepy."

"Okay, what is going on in here?" questioned Mr. Smith.

"We were playing a scary game and Pumpkin got scared and ran," Asa offered.

"Dad! That's not true! There is a man out there sitting in the tree! He has one big, fat, greasy tooth, with yellow pants, and his face changes colors! Dad, I seen it myself, and he has a crooked cane! Look out the window!" Pumpkin yelled.

"Elliot that is absolutely ridiculous!" said Mr. Smith.

"Dad, mom, look and see! Open the curtain!" Pumpkin insisted.

CHAPTER 7

"Let me look," offered Uncle Marcus.

Pumpkin scrambled behind his parents as Uncle Marcus walked over to the window. Tana and Asa sat frozen on the bed with Tana squeezing her eyes tightly shut. He ripped opened the curtains, and of course there was nothing out there but the trees in the backyard blowing in the wind. When everyone stood there in silence Pumpkin's mom could see her son really believed what he saw. As Uncle Marcus helped Pumpkin's dad close and lock the window closing the curtain, Asa and Tana sat still trying to put on a brave front.

"Do you really think someone was out there?" Mom asked.

"Mom, dad, I know that creepy guy is out there! Asa and Tana saw him!" Pumpkin replied.

Asa and Tana just sat there with this dumb look on their faces.

"We're sorry Pumpkin, but we didn't mean to scare you. Mr. Smith, we pointed to the trees outside and told Pumpkin the creepy guy was out there, and I guess Pumpkin was so scared he thought he saw something," Asa answered with an innocent look on his face.

"Okay, that is enough for tonight, all of you get ready for bed," warned Mr. Smith.

"Tana I can make your bed in the other room," Mrs. Smith suggested.

"Oh no! Could I sleep on the floor with the guys? I am not use to sleeping in new places," Tana pleaded with desparation.

"Well, wouldn't you like a room to yourself instead of being around these boys?" asked Mrs. Smith.

"Nah, we camp out on the floor at home when we are bored. It's okay with me," Asa said.

"Pumpkin?" Mrs. Smith asked.

Pumpkin wanted to say, 'heck no,' but everyone was staring at him.

"Yeah, whatever," Pumpkin responded with a hateful look at his friends.

Pumpkin was so mad he was spittin bullets! He knew what he saw, and now he feels like a dummy in front of everybody. What else could he do? Those two were believable enough even he began thinking maybe he did imagine it.

"I'll be back with pajamas for you Tana," offered Mrs. Smith.

"Thank you Mrs. Smith," Tana replied.

As Pumpkin's parents and Uncle walked out the room, no sooner than the door closed Pumpkin turned on Asa and Tana hissing like a snake!

"You guys are liars! Why did you do that?!! If I could kick you out of my room I would right now!" Pumpkin yelled.

"Pumpkin! Shut up! We could not tell your parents, because I looked out the window again while you were running for your parents! He was gone, and we all know how parents are if they don't see anything. See how quick they believed me. Grownups never believe us kids," Asa responded with fright.

"Well, Asa we were caught telling fibs a couple of times to mom and dad."

"I know Tana, but his parents believed us a lot sooner than Pumpkin."

"Well I don't like looking like an idiot!" replied Pumpkin.

"Too late," Tana whispered under her breath.

"You lucky I am nice! Else I would put you out! Matter of fact, you two are creeping me out. You sit there like two zombies staring at me, grinning like we are playing for fun!" Pumpkin yelled.

"Will you two stop it" Asa yelled.

"No I will not! You guys were wrong, and you made me look stupid."

"I'm sorry Pumpkin, I just thought. Oh never mind! But, I rather look stupid than have that thing in here!" Asa suggested.

Pumpkin sat down on his bed next to the brother and sister leaning over with his head in his hands. After a few minutes with no one speaking, and only the ticking of the clock on the wall Pumpkin was finally giving up. He looked up at Asa and Tana.

"Okay, okay! Then what are we going to do?" asked Pumpkin.

"I don't know Pumpkin. But I would like to know how I saw his face that close to the window, and we are on the second floor," wondered Asa.

"Oh my goodness, I didn't even think about that. I never saw him, because you screamed Asa. I stayed on the floor. Pumpkin, did you really see anything?" Tana asked hoping Pumpkin was calmer.

"Well, no," Pumpkin replied.

"Then why did you tell your parents you saw him?"asked Tana.

"Because I did! I saw him when you two knocked on my door falling into my house!"

"Look guys, we have to sit and figure this out. I say we get ready for bed," Asa suggested.

"Are you crazy?!! Who wants to go to bed?" Pumpkin asked, incredulous.

"This is just to make sure your parents see we are listening, and they won't keep bothering us," Asa explained.

"Good plan brother," Tana said.

"Thanks," said Asa.

Pumpkin wanted to throw up watching these two patting each other on the back like they did something. He was still madder than mad so he mocked Tana in a high pitch voice.

"Good plan brother. Thanks," mocked Pumpkin.

"Oh be quiet Pumpkin!" shouted Tana.

The knock on the door made all three of them jump. Mrs. Smith came into the room carrying blankets, pillows, and a pair of pajamas for Tana. She could hear them on the other side of the door, but she refused to get in the middle of their little spat. She knew kids will be friends after their arguments.

Opening the door Mrs. Smith faced Tana. "Okay Tana, these are Pumpkin's older sister pajamas. She won't mind, because she is at college. They will be big on you, but you will be fine. By the way, did you tell your mom you two will be home tomorrow after breakfast?" Mrs. Smith asked.

"Uh, yes ma'am. Asa talked to mom before we ate dinner. She said that was fine with her. We promised her we would not be any trouble," Tana replied.

"Oh you two are just fine, and Pumpkin needs to have more friends. Well, here are blankets, sheets, and pillows for you two. I want the lights out in twenty minutes," warned Mrs. Smith.

"Okay, mom."

Pumpkin knew what his mom meant. She did not like Scooter, because he picked on other kids. That was a big no no in her book, but he felt sorry for him, because Scooter did not have any friends. He could see Scooter did not know how to be friends with anyone. So, Pumpkin thought why not try and help him out. Pumpkin thought back in his mind when he saw Scooter on the playground on the first day of school. He remembered he had asked him if he wanted to play catch. Being typical Scooter, he gave him a mean and nasty look. Eventually he nodded yes after looking around and seeing that no one would talk to him. Pumpkin felt that was a million years ago, and that's how his crazy friendship with Scooter began.

Basil: "Well, good for Pumpkin! I think. Who wants to be friends with a bully?"

After Mrs. Smith left the room Tana turned and spoke to Pumpkin. "Boy that was close with your mom. I just went blank in the head. Do you think your mother believed us?"

"Yeah, that's because she likes you two," offered Pumpkin.

"Well, where's the bathroom? I am so tired," asked Asa.

As those kids were getting ready for bed there sure was something going on in that backyard! The three of them did not hear anything, because they were so busy chatting it up. After much discussion everyone gave their opinion, but no one came up with any answers.

Basil: "They're thinking so much their brains probably hurt them from all that concentrating."

"Hey guys, we have to come up with a plan, but we have to put our heads together about what just happened," Pumpkin whispered.

"Yeah you're right," Asa agreed.

"Tell me from the beginning what happened to you guys with this creepy thing."

Asa and Tana started from the beginning when they first encountered the stranger in the park. Tana filled in the blanks finishing the rest of their story.

"Are you kidding? Let me get this straight. This guy appears out at the edge of the park, and he has been chasing you guys since! It sounds like he could have snatched you when you were at the park with me and Scooter, but he didn't."

"Yes! That's right! Asa, remember when you turned around at the park, and he was standing there with me next to you! Even when mom floated up the stairs behind us she could have reached out, and grabbed us. Why didn't she?" asked Tana.

"Wait a minute, your mom... floated up the stairs?" wondered Pumpkin beginning to get scared all over again.

"Now you see why we can't go home," Tana stated.

"Now that we put our heads together there is one thing I know, and that is that creepy man wants me, and Tana," said Asa.

Basil: "DUH-UHH!"

"Look, we got to get out of here early tomorrow," Pumpkin responded.

"And do what?" asked Asa.

"I don't know! But we have to see Scooter, and find out what happened to him," Pumpkin replied with hope.

"He's right Asa," Tana agreed hoping her brother did as well.

On that note all three rushed to finish getting ready for bed, and when they finally snuggled under their covers from the cold air condition, and started to think of what they needed to do they felt a little better about tomorrow.

"Now that we figured out that thing wants us, how can we go anywhere without it finding us?" asked Asa.

"First of all, he wants you two. Also, we got to figure out how Scooter disappeared," Pumpkin suggested.

"I think the weather has something to do with it. Don't you notice there are always dark clouds, and the wind kicks up right before he comes?" Tana asked.

"Yeah! As soon as I saw those clouds, and heard that wind I slammed the door shut! The weather was always bad when he showed up at the park too!" Asa noted.

"I remember downtown as well. He stuck his head out from behind the car with that icky smile," Tana shuddered.

"Now that I think about it Tana, it goes quiet just before something happens," Asa recalled.

"What do you mean?" Tana asked.

"Remember when we were hiding under the table at home?" Asa asked.

"Yes, I remember."Tana answered with a tremble in her voice.

"Do you remember how quiet it got, while mom and dad were at the front door"? recalled Asa.

"Oh I forgot about that! But what does that mean?" asked Tana.

"Yeah, what does that mean?" Pumpkin piped up.

"I don't know. I just know these things keep happening when he is around, or just before he shows up," said Asa.

Basil: "Well, well. They are finally getting their act together trying to figure this thing out."

"Look, let's get up early and eat before we go. I will tell mom we are going over to your place to get ready for the softball game at the park," Pumpkin chimed in.

"There's a game at the park tomorrow?" asked Tana.

"Yeah, I'm playing with my team," Pumpkin replied.

"At that same park!" Tana exclaimed.

"No! It's the park on the other side of town. My parents will not make it, because mom is dragging dad around shopping for clothes," Pumpkin said.

"So, we should eat, and then we should head straight for Scooter's house," said Asa.

"Do you guys think Scooter is like that thing?" wondered Pumpkin.

"You think so?" asked Tana.

"It could be. Look, all we have to do is knock on the door, and when Scooter comes to the door we will know," replied Asa.

"We will know what? Until he opens his mouth and if a big tooth appears then we run!" Pumpkin said.

"I don't know, but we gotta go over there and find out," suggested Asa.

"Asa, the word is got, not gotta," Tana corrected.

Pumpkin rolled his eyes at Tana's remark. 'Boy', he thought. 'She thinks she knows everything'.

"I guess better in the daylight than the dark," Pumpkin offered.

"Hey Pumpkin, do you usually call Scooter's house in the morning, or do you talk at all at night?" asked Tana.

"What are you getting at Tana?" asked Asa.

"Ah man! That's right! We always talk when I get home, or he calls me about school," Pumpkin replied.

"Does he usually call in the morning?" Tana asked.

"Yeah, because there is my game tomorrow, and he would want to meet there. That's because he has a crush on Lottie Martin. She always comes to the games, because her brother plays on my team. So he always asks me what he could do to get her to notice him."

"So, he has not called tonight, maybe he will tomorrow," said Asa.

"We will see. Hey, what should I say to him if he calls?" asked Pumpkin.

"Tell him you will meet him at the game. Don't we want to make sure he is normal, and if he's not, at least we will be around a bunch of people at the ball game," Tana suggested.

"That's true. Pumpkin, we have to make sure he does not feel we are on to him... Pumpkin?"

"Sheesh! He's snoring like a bull Asa!"

"So much for being scared" Asa said with little hope.

"We should look out the window Asa."

"Why? If he's there what are we going to do? We just lied to Pumpkin's parents, and his uncle. And if I see that face up against the window Tana I will lose my marbles."

"What does that mean?" Tana asked with frustration.

"Tana, I will lose my dinner and my mind if I see that thing again in the dark."

"Oh, okay" Tana replied.

Too tired to talk, Asa and Tana fell asleep within minutes.

Basil: "Look out the window!! Boy, I wish they would have looked out that window."

CHAPTER 8

A few hours later there was a scratching sound crawling up the side of the house. Butch the dog was going crazy outside barking, but no one heard Butch because they had fallen asleep, and Pumpkin's parent's bedroom was on the other side of the house. Also, the strong winds blowing against the house muffled his barks. Butch was always in the dog house in the back of the house at night. Aaah, but Pumpkin heard something as he came out of his deep sleep. He heard his dog Butch barking. Pumpkin also heard that scratching on the side of the house; he looked over, and saw Tana and Asa sleeping on the floor. His tongue was stuck in his throat, and nothing came out. Not even a squeak. But he did notice the curtain lifted on its own suddenly slid open. Wait a minute thought Pumpkin, how can his curtain open from the inside, and that creature was outside! And there he was his face right up smack against the window, and staring at Asa and Tana. Even though it was dark with the bright moon shining behind the stranger Pumpkin noticed that big, fat, greasy tooth hanging over his lip.

"Eeew," Pumpkin whispered.

That's when the crazy looking creepy man turned, and looked at him. He heard Pumpkin even though Pumpkin barely whispered the word. He just continued staring, but he wouldn't say a word. Pumpkin silently started crying, wishing for his mama, but he couldn't move because he was soooo scared. Then the curtains slowly closed. The scratching sound faded away. Pumpkin was so scared he really talked himself into thinking it was a dream.

Basil: "But it wasn't, he,he,he. What, what now?"

Pumpkin woke up the next morning looking out the window from his bed at a clear morning with not a cloud in the sky. Suddenly Pumpkin bolted straight up out of his bed sitting there not able to move. He remembered last night, and the more he thought about it, it began to dawn on him it was not a dream. But more like a nightmare. Worst of all, he remembered those curtains were closed when that stranger left. Oh boy thought Pumpkin, he felt sick to his stomach. Sitting up in his bed he called to Asa and Tana.

"Tana, Asa, wake up!" Pumpkin shouted.

Asa felt groggy, and terribly tired, and he also forgot where he was sleeping.

"Why!" Asa asked.

"Why? Because I saw yuck mouth last night! That's why!" Pumpkin replied.

Basil: "Bet that woke them up!"

Asa and Tana both sat up like someone hit them. Slowly the events from last night began to come back to them.

"You saw it!? How, what happened?" Asa wondered.

"I heard scratching sounds, but it was Butch's barking that woke me up. Then suddenly the curtains opened," Pumpkin said.

"The curtains opened by itself?" Asa asked with wide eyes.

"You think I ran over there and opened it like superman! Yes, the curtains opened on its own. That's when I saw him, and he just stared at you two. He even heard me when I whispered 'eeew'," explained Pumpkin.

Basil: "Yikers!"

"That thing has yuck mouth! I was so scared I couldn't move. Then the curtains closed, and he was gone," Pumpkin said.

"Whoa! So that thing was just staring at us while we were sleeping! Ick!!" Asa said in disgust.

"I think I want to throw up," Tana said.

"You better not!" Pumpkin said.

"What did you do Pumpkin when you saw him?" asked Asa.

"Nothing. He just stared at me then he was gone."

"How creepy! That thing staring at us while we were sleeping! Wait a minute, what happened to Butch?" asked Tana.

The three of them ran to the window so fast they forgot about the creepy stranger being out there. Pumpkin tore the curtain open further, and there was Butch sitting there looking up at them, like he was waiting for them. There was only one problem with this picture. Butch somehow made it out the dog house, and tied to the fence with huge footprints leading up over the wood fence out the yard. Tana and Asa stared at Butch from the window, and Pumpkin shaking like a leaf behind them. Pumpkin figured they might as well hear the rest of the story, because he did not want to think of this problem by himself.

"Guys, that's not all," Pumpkin began.

Tana did not want to ask, but she did. "What is it?."

"When he left, the curtains closed, but when I woke up this morning the curtains were wide open," Pumpkin explained.

Asa was losing his cool quickly. "Whoa! You are not kidding?"

"Does a chicken have lips?" asked Pumpkin.

There was a knock on the door, and all three of them jumped and screamed. Mrs. Smith walked in the room, and she could see her son was really hamming it up with this scared routine, she just could not believe Pumpkin's story.

"What is it with you three? Ah, I bet it was those scary stories you told each other," Mrs. Smith recalled with a smile.

"Yeah, mom what's for breakfast?"

"Why it's your favorite. You know you always eat pancakes and bacon before your game."

"That sounds real good Mrs. Smith. I am starvin like Marvin!" Tana said.

"Well, you guys wash up, and come downstairs, because breakfast will be done in a few minutes," offered Mrs.Smith.

"Starvin like Marvin? What's up with that?" asked Pumpkin.

"I don't know, I heard my dad say it one day," replied Tana.

Tana didn't know about Asa, but she missed her parents even though they were creepy. She just wanted to go home and be a kid again.

Basil: "NOT."

Although they were scared it did not stopped them from getting ready for breakfast. The three washed up, got dressed and headed downstairs to eat. Once Pumpkin saw the pancakes you would never have thought he saw anything scary last night. Asa and Tana were a little nervous, because they had to figure out where they were going to go tonight if their home was still creeped out with their parents. But good old Pumpkin kept the conversation going with his Uncle Marcus about his softball game.

"So, what position do you play?" inquired Uncle Marcus.

"I play short stop today. Sometimes I have to pitch, but that's okay I'm not that bad."

"I have to go down to the office, but if I am done early I will come down and check you out," said Uncle Marcus.

"That would be great, because we need a cheering section for our team" added Asa.

Tana and Pumpkin looked at Asa, trying to figure out what was he up to. It didn't matter, because they were both too wound up to figure out why. Pumpkin jumped up from the table ready to play ball, and if that is what will get his mind off of what is happening then so be it.

"I'm done eating, are you guys ready?" asked Pumpkin.

"We have to clean up the room," said Asa.

"We? We who? Clean the room? What's wrong with you? Are you crazy?" Pumpkin asked with disbelief.

"No I am not, that's the least we can do," said Asa.

Rolling her eyes Tana looked at both of them arguing."Come on guys, so we can hurry up and go to the park"

Mrs Smith wondered why her son could not be this responsible. "Wow, Elliot I think you can learn a few things with these two. Don't worry about it he will get in there and straighten things up later."

Asa sweetly replied. "That's okay Mrs. Smith we can do it. Right, Pumpkin?"

With a look to kill, Pumpkin answered "Yeah, whatever." .

Tana rolled her eyes again at Pumpkin. "The word is, yes."

"Nooo, the word is, shut up. Know that word?" Pumpkin sneered.

Basil: "No, that's two words. Know how to count?"

Mom had enough of the arguing between them. "Okay, that's enough you two. Well then, we will get going with our shopping. Elliot, don't forget to feed Butch. Dear, are you ready to go?"

"Yes, I'm ready. I have a feeling this will be a long day. Let's go dear, so I will meet you out at the car," Mr. Smith replied.

As soon as they were in Pumpkin's room with the door safely shut, Asa held his stomach, and started laughing.

"I wish you could have seen your face! It was funny when I said we will clean up the room," Asa laughed falling on the bed.

"What is wrong with you? I like my room just the way it is, messy. Just in case my parents look for me they can't find me in here. I have done it before, and I like it that way," Pumpkin retorted.

"Well, we at least have to pick up the blankets and stuff. My parents would kill us if they found out we left this mess for your mother," Tana added with authority.

"If it makes you happy, then knock yourself out. I will be downstairs waiting so hurry up."

Pumpkin was anxious to get out of the house, and do something normal. Staying in the house another minute would make his head explode as he headed out the bedroom. Running downstairs leaving Asa and Tana in his room folding the blankets was fine with him, as long as he did not have to do it.

Folding the blankets Tana said, "Asa, we have to go home today, and see what is at our house. You and I both know Pumpkin is real shaky when it comes to anything that scares him."

"You can't blame him Tana. I wouldn't go back there either, but it is our home. We have to see if our parents are there. Let's just go, and maybe we can think of something. We have all day to figure this one out. Instead of looking for him at the game, we have to get to Scooter and see what's going on with him."

Yelling from downstairs Pumpkin was ready to go.

"Hey, I finish feeding Butch, come on you guys! Let's go!"

"We're coming!" Asa replied.

Oh it was such a beautiful day in the little town of Seward. The sky was clear, and the birds were singing. Let's see how long this last. Once they decided to go to Scooter's house they were determine to fight back. Those three kids were on a mission, and they were going to find out who was this funny looking guy, and why was he chasing them. It must be a beautiful day, because all three of them acted like they did not have a care in the world. But they were really trying to figure out what to do with Scooter if he answered the door. They headed out the front door with big ideas on how to catch the stranger. Walking through town all three came up with many more ideas on how to knock on the door if Scooter answered.

"How will we know if Scooter is normal when he answers the door?" Tana wondered.

Asa answered his sister with a serious tone. "If he doesn't have a wet looking tooth hanging out over his lip. Remember, mom had one after she answered the door with dad."

"Did your dad have one?" asked Pumpkin.

Thinking about that night Asa answered with a shudder. "We don't know, because we never looked him in the face after he answered the door with mom. Tana and I ran in our room, and locked the door so we were by ourselves. Remember, they were acting strange, and we just heard our dad on the other side of the door."

Pumpkin looked at them in awe. "Now that is spooky. I'm glad I ran home, and that creepy guy wants you two."

"Thanks a lot Pumpkin. That sure makes me feel better," Tana responded with a look of disgust.

Pumpkin realized that was dumb. "Sorry, but I just get the creeps when I think about it."

Asa was lost, and he did not want to think about their parents. "Pumpkin, we are practically on the other side of town, where is Scooter's house? We have been walking for a while."

"There it is at the end of the block," Pumpkin pointed out.

Basil: "What a cute house, even though a bully lives there. Boy you would never think Scooter would live anywhere nice. For a person like him maybe a cave is more like it."

"Okay, what do I say to him?" Pumpkin asked.

Asa could see the change in his friend even though he could not blame him, but they had to stick to the plan. "Pumpkin you are not going to chicken out on us? You are looking mighty sweaty, and you haven't done anything! He is not going to be suspicious, because he knows you have a game today, right?"

"Well I guess so. But he didn't call me last night, and we don't know what he looks like since he disappeared at the park. He could look like a monster, and snatch us right off the porch! Now that I think about it guys, I am not feeling too good, and maybe we should skip Scooter," Pumpkin answered with regret.

Tana had to think of something quick to keep Pumpkin focused from his fear. "Sure, then he will come looking for you when you are all by yourself. Then what are you going to do? At least we are here with you in broad daylight."

Basil: "It took all of a second to think that one over."

Pumpkin did not want to run away, and the more he thought about it he wanted to get this over with. After a few minutes of pumping himself up, with determination and gumption he was ready to go. And the other reason was Tana and Asa was breathing down his back.

"Come on, let's go!" Pumpkin said with all the braveness of a lion.

When all of them reached the front door to Scooter's house Pumpkin felt like he was dizzy. His stomach began to turn into knots. Now he really did feel sick.

Basil: "Oh sure! Look at Pumpkin. He sure looks like he is hanging back and ready to run!"

Running out of patience Tana urged him on. "Pumpkin, will you get up here and knock on the door! Come on! We can't knock on the door for you; if we did then he will be really suspicious. Come on, knock on the door!"

Basil: "Yeah, knock on the door Pumpkin!"

"Okay, okay I need a second! But I am telling you both, if I see one inch of a wet looking tooth I am outta here. I will leave you two! Got it?" Pumpkin said shaking at the knees.

"Like we didn't know that before; Knock on the door!" Asa yelled.

Basil: "He, he,he. Look at Pumpkin sweat."

"Okay! I heard you!" Pumpkin yelled.

Basil: "Look how he squares his shoulders back, and sticks out his chest...like a chicken! That boy is so, so scared. He, he, he. Go on Pumpkin, knock on the door!

Pumpkin sucks in air, and finally knocks on the door. The door swung open so fast all three of them screamed. Pumpkin was already down the sidewalk yelling like a hyena! All you saw was the back of his baseball uniform with the number eight on his back fading away down the street. Asa and Tana tried to run, but they fell over each other again when the door swung open. When they looked up they were staring at a short woman with an awfully mean look on her face.

"Oh my, hello there. I am so sorry. I thought you were someone else. Someone keeps tapping on my door, but when I go to answer it no one is there," Mrs. Walker said to the three kids.

Mrs. Walker was not happy, and if she could catch the little imps who were banging on her door she was going to give them a what for. Hands over her eyes squinting from the sun she could see the back of Pumpkin's uniform running down the sidewalk.

"Is that Pumpkin running down the street?" asked Mrs. Walker. *'Hmm, now why would he knock on the door then run'* thought Mrs. Walker?

Coming from behind his mom, Scooter was ready to beat up whoever was knocking on their door. Meanwhile, Asa and Tana picked themselves up off the ground, and dusted themselves off feeling foolish. After watching Pumpkin take off, Asa felt their plans were totally forgotten.

"Who is it mom?" Scooter asked.

"Oh I'm sorry. What are your names?" inquired Mrs. Walker.

"Hi, my name is Tana, and this is my brother Asa," replied Tana.

"Well hi there. I guess you two came to see Henry," said Mrs. Walker.

"Henry? Who's Henry?" asked Asa.

Looking at Asa and Tana through his beady little eyes Scooter was ready to punch whoever was making his mom mad by banging on their front door. Now they knew his real name, well, let's say Scooter was not pleased.

Coming up behind his mother Scooter barked out, "That's me, why are you going to make something of it?" Scooter retorted.

"Umm, no," Asa replied with a lump in his throat.

"Be nice dear. Well, I will leave you three alone," said Mrs. Walker.

Mrs. Walker turns around and heads down the hallway, she did not have time to catch who was banging on her door. After all, she needed to be at her hair appointment. Heading down the hallway Mrs. Walker yelled over her shoulder back at her son.

"Invite them inside Henry; I don't want flies in the house."

Basil: "Well looky here. Guess who comes running up like nothing happened. Yep, our fearless guy Pumpkin!"

Once Pumpkin saw Scooter from down the block, and Asa and Tana were not screaming in fear he decided to go back and see what was going on with his friend Scooter. That mad dash down the block really had him breathing hard when he came up and answered Asa.

"Hey Pumpkin, did you hurt yourself running?" asked Asa.

"No, not really," replied Pumpkin.

"Why were you running down the street?" Scooter asked.

"He was trying to find his courage," answered Asa.

"Funny," retorted Pumpkin.

"What's going on Pumpkin? And why are these two here?" Scooter asked with a sneer on his face.

Pumpkin stared at his friend, "You know why, and we have to talk Scooter. Are you coming to the game today?"

"Yeah, I called you a while ago at home, but there was no answer. I know we have to talk, and I am scared to death," replied Scooter.

Tana was going to correct Scooter's grammar until she heard him say he was 'scared.'

Basil: "Oh wait a minute! Scooter just came out and said he was scared! In front of people! And in front of a girl no less! Now everyone was scared, because Scooter is the bully!!! He is not scared of anything! NOT!"

Scooter turns around yelling down the hall at his mother.

"Mom, I'm going to the softball game!!"

Yelling from the kitchen Mrs. Walker was glad her little Scooter had friends to play with.

"Don't you be late again like the last time, or you will be grounded again. Only worse!! Do you hear me Henry?" Mrs. Walker asked.

"Yes mom!" Scooter answered rolling his eyes.

Basil: "Henry? Hennnry! That name sure does not fit him! He's too mean to have that kind of name. Maybe that's why he's a bully."

Once they all left Scooter's house, and headed for the field Scooter threatened each and every one of them if they so much as blabbed about his real name. Asa was not going to take that from Scooter, even though he was the school bully.

"You got a lot of nerve! We came over here to make sure you were all right!" yelled Asa.

"And to make sure you don't have one tooth in your mouth," added Pumpkin.

"This is the thanks we get?" Tana chimed in.

Scooter was taken by surprise by all of them ganging up on him. Everybody was supposed to be scared of him, what just happened here?

'Oh well' he thought, he had too many other things on his mind to be worried about these dweebs. Quietly he followed the group down the sidewalk thinking his stomach was not feeling well, and his feet were killing him.

Pumpkin felt restless and scared. "Come on guys lets go, I don't want to be late else the coach will bench me. Hey Asa, why did you tell my Uncle Marcus we need a cheering section for my team?"

Shrugging his shoulders Asa replied, "Just in case anything happens, at least we have an adult to help us."

" Asa, that's nice, but what could his Uncle Marcus do?"

"I don't know, but he could help us. We can only do so much as kids. If he sees this thing chasing us he could tell other adults and then they may believe us," Asa replied.

"I never thought of that," Tana replied.

"Okay Scooter, what happened to you? One minute you were on the merry go round, and the next thing I know I see you disappear," questioned Pumpkin.

Scooter takes a noticeable deep breath while walking behind them, and explains what had happened to him.

"I can't explain it. One minute I am on the merry go round, the next minute I am opening the door to my house," Scooter answered.

"But you disappeared at the park in the day time, and your mom told us you just got home and it was late! You don't live that far from the park," Tana noted.

"All I know is I did not see anything until I was facing my front door," Scooter said while shaking from the memory.

"Do you remember the time you got home?" Asa asked.

"Yeah, it was around nine thirty. That I know, because mom kept yelling at me the time I came in. Mom says she called all my friends."

Basil: "That must have been one quick call. Bullies don't have friends!"

Scooter was becoming visibly upset. "Finally my mom and dad started to go look for me when I didn't come home."

Basil: "Hmmm, once again, Scooter has friends?"

Pumpkin started thinking. "Wait a minute, I ran from the park around five thirty and dinner was ready at home. I know that, because mom always has dinner on the table by then."

Basil: "Okay, somebody do the math!"

"So, that means you were gone for over four hours!!" noted Tana.

Basil: "Good job girl!"

"What in the world happened to you all that time?!!" exclaimed Tana.

"I don't know! I don't remember anything. I lied in bed all that night shaking, and wondering what happened. Then I heard like a scratching sound on the side of the house, but I was too scared to go look out the window," Scooter whispered with fear.

Basil: "Wanna see three people turn to stone? Look at them!"

All three kids stood rock still standing on the sidewalk listening to Scooter.

Scooter continued in a shaky voice, "So I ran to my big brother's room and hung out with him until I fell asleep on the floor."

"Yeah, when it started to get louder, and the sound became closer that's when I took off to my brother's room. I wasn't staying around to find out. When I went back to my room this morning the window was open. Scooter looked at the others reaction to his story." Scooter could see the look of fear in all three of his friends. "Why? Did this happen to you?"

Suddenly, Tana caught on to something. "Yes, it happened to us as well. Wait a minute, your window was opened?"

"Yeah," Scooter replied.

Basil: "Oh looky, look. Looks like Scooter wants to scoot right back home! I think his face is beginning to turn colors too. He, he, he. Who's the brave one now? I guess all that bullying isn't what it's cracked up to be. If I remember correctly, he wasn't scared of anyone! Hmmm, I wonder if that's what you get for being mean to people."

Hearing all of this made Pumpkin want to run for the hills. "Hey guys, we are close to the park, and we still haven't figured out what's going on. Let's meet afterwards, and get a sound game plan going."

Asa agreed. "We have to, because sis and I can't go home. Come on guys let's go over to the bleachers to watch the game from there."

Heading for the bleachers Scooter never thought about Lottie Martin. The game was going smoothly, and the crowd was cheering, and rooting for their team. Except for those three kids watching. They were watching alright. They were watching those trees at the edge of the field! Scooter was so scared he wasn't bullying the kids on the other team.

Basil: "Now that's scared!"

"Do you think he will show up at this park?" Tana whispered.

Scooter answered, "I hope not. He was one ugly looking dude. All I know is I just felt funny. One minute I was cold, and then I was hot. My head was spinning like a top."

Once the game was over the park started clearing out, because Pumpkin's team was winning easily. All the people that were left were the losing team players, and they were ready to leave. Asa and Tana were not feeling too easy once the game was over. Anywhere with trees made them want to be somewhere else. Asa asked himself, 'what are they going to do?' Pumpkin could see his friends were deep in thought as he was running up the bleachers to sit with them.

"Well guys that was fun. I think I just might go for the major leagues. You have to admit that was good pitching I did. Did you see Sherrie Daniels staring at me, and smiling? Boy I am good!!" beamed Pumpkin.

"You know, I really think something is wrong with you Pumpkin. Here we are in the middle of a scary time, and you are bragging about a girl staring at you," Tana screeched.

"Well it's better than thinking about it!! I get the hee bee jee bees thinking about that tooth, and that face! You did not see what I saw last night. Yikes! Send me on a one way ticket to Mars if I can get away from that thing!" Pumpkin answered shaking his head.

Tana replied with little patience, "At least you didn't go through what Scooter been through. Right, Scooter?"

Tana turns towards Scooter waiting for his reply.

"Huh?" Scooter asked. Scooter turns toward Tana with a smile on his face when he heard Tana call his name.

"Scooter? No! Oh my goodness gracious! Your tooth! You only have one tooth in your mouth!" exclaimed Tana.

Tana immediately slides back along the bleachers, and looks Scooter over. Looking down she sees his feet had changed as well. When Tana took a good look at his feet, and that one tooth in his mouth she wanted to faint.

"And look at your feet! Your feet are huge!" marveled Pumpkin.

"Oh monkey buns! Scooter! What's wrong with you?" Asa asked.

That was all the three of them needed to see, and of course Pumpkin was already in first gear running the other way.

Scooter had a smile on his face, and he looked at them with a creepy looking sneer. "Come here guys. I have to ask you something."

Scooter started sliding down the bleachers like he was floating towards them. Tana was disgusted and frighten looking at Scooter, but she could not move at first. When Scooter opened his mouth all Tana could see was one big tooth. That was all she needed to get away from Scooter.

CHAPTER 9

Basil: "Has anyone seen Pumpkin?"

Pumpkin had already retreated as he was watching Asa and Tana slowly backing up talking to Scooter. After getting a glimpse of that tooth in Scooter's mouth Pumpkin was gone! Getting a safe distance down the street Pumpkin turns and yells at Asa and Tana.

"RUN! RUN!" yelled Pumpkin.

"Come on Tana!" Asa yelled. Asa snatched Tana's hand, and ran for dear life. It's a miracle they didn't fall down those bleachers. They couldn't catch up with Pumpkin, because he was fast!

Basil: "I told you that kid can run."

Even as they were running Asa managed to turn around. All he saw was this lone figure sitting on the bleachers. It was Scooter, waving at them like a final goodbye.

Basil: "YIKERS!"

"Wait, Tana! Slow down! Look at the park!" yelled Asa.

Breathing hard Tana turns around, and there was Scooter waving to them with the dark clouds over head and raining. Now isn't that something, Scooter was waving to them like there was nothing wrong.

Basil: "Egad! Call the cops!"

Pointing at Scooter, Tana yells, "There he goes down the bleachers. He's floating down the bleachers! Look at his feet!"

"Where are all those people from the other team? They were just there!" observed Asa.

Pumpkin doubles back to Asa and Tana out of breath.

"No, the last car left when you turned to talk to Scooter. I said good bye to that team when they were leaving," said Pumpkin.

"Where do you think he's going?" questioned Asa.

"Hopefully, to his creepy house and not mine!" Pumpkin said.

"What happened? And when did he change?" asked Tana.

"I bet it was when he left his window opened! I bet that thing crawled through the window, and turned him into a monster too! That's got to be it!" yelled Pumpkin.

Tana could not believe it. "But he was normal with us."

"Or was he?" added Asa.

"Okay you two, now what are we going to do? This whole entire town will end up with one big tooth!" Pumpkin squeaked.

"Keep walking guys, even though it is sunny we are the only ones on the sidewalk," Asa noticed with dread.

"You don't have to tell me twice. Should we go to my house?" asked Pumpkin.

"We should go to his house to see if he's there," suggested Asa.

"What! Are you crazy! Look, if you want to be a hero then go for it! I am heading home to get away from all of this! Why are you running TO trouble?!!!" yelled Pumpkin.

"That's because IT is coming after us! I rather we figure it out, and get him first before he gets us!" Asa answered back.

Pumpkin had it with these two, and he was going to let them have it. "There you go again with US! There ain't no us!!! Us is you and that sister of yours! Us has nothing to do with me! I'm outta here!"

Basil: "No grammar correction there!

Pumpkin walks away with Asa and Tana watching him walk down the sidewalk. As he walks away Tana yells at him from behind.

"Pumpkin, are you really going to leave us by ourselves?!!" Tana asked.

Pumpkin did not turn around, but he answered Tana as he continued down the sidewalk.

"You're not by yourselves, you have each other!" replied Pumpkin.

Asa began yelling down the sidewalk after Pumpkin, because he knew him and his sister could not go back home. And they were way past desperate.

"Pumpkin, we have no place to go!" Asa pleaded.

Pumpkin stops with his back to them for a few seconds.

Tana did not care how she begged, she was past scared. "Please Pumpkin, don't leave us! You are all we got!"

Pumpkin whirls around grumbling and mumbling under his breath heading back down the sidewalk toward Asa and Tana angrily pointing his finger at the brother and sister.

"I better not get eaten by this thing! If I am it's your fault!" warned Pumpkin.

Asa was so thankful Pumpkin changed his mind he wanted to hug him, but he knew better.

"Thanks," said Asa.

"Yeah, whatever," said Pumpkin.

Tana nearly corrected Pumpkin, but she thought better of it.

Tana timidly suggested, "I think we need to go by our house too. It's still daylight,"

"WHAT! ARE YOU BOTH CRAZY?!!!" yelled Pumpkin.

Basil: "Yes, they are related!"

"Why did I even ask? Because both of you are nuts!!! Geez Louise!!"

"Pumpkin. Look, we have to go back to our house to see what is going on! We just can't ignore we don't live there! Do you have any ideas?" asked Asa.

"Yeah, go home! So, are you ready to go knock on your door, and see who answers it?" Pumpkin asked.

"He's right Asa, because I'm not going up to that door either," now that I think about it Tana replied.

"Then how are we going to find out who's in there?" wondered Asa.

After a few minutes of thinking Pumpkin came up with an idea.

"Hey! What if we send some unsuspecting kid to knock on the door and see who answers the door!"

"What if they snatch him? We can't do that!" replied Tana.

Pumpkin was on a roll. "Not if he stands far enough away from the door after he knocks. Let's get a kid a little older than us who is smart enough to run, and then he could run if he sees something crazy looking."

"How are we going to get someone to do it?" Asa asked.

"I don't know. Let me think for a second."

"What if we tell this person some sob story, and pay them," suggested Tana.

"Pay them with what Tana? We don't have any money," Asa re minded her with a grim look on his face.

After listening to his friends go back and forth, and wanting to get rid of that monster Pumpkin finally fessed up.

"Okay, okay! I have some money, but you two will pay me back! I have ten dollars," said Pumpkin.

Basil: "If you believe Pumpkin has ten dollars, then I love looking at big greasy teeth! That scoundrel has twenty dollars on him."

"Wait a minute, why are you being so nice?" asked Asa.

"Two reasons: One, the both of you will pay me back. Two, if that means there's a chance we can get this thing out of here then I am willing to give up my borrowed bucks! Remember, borrowed," said Pumpkin.

"Well, let's find someone. I'm sure we will run across someone by the time we get to our house," said Asa.

Basil: "Oh boy! Aren't they smart! Well let's see how smart they are. Any bets on Pumpkin? What will he do if anything scary opens that door?"

The kids began walking in the neighborhood to Asa and Tana's house looking for someone to knock on the door. They were hopeful someone would be crazy enough to pull it off. It was getting late, and most kids were already home.

"Hey, how about that kid over there?" suggested Tana.

"Are you kidding? That's Arnold, old man Harry's grandson. He screams louder than old man Harry. He gets mad just looking at you. Let's keep looking," suggested Pumpkin.

They walk some more through town looking over other kids who were either too little, or too fat to run anywhere. Tana wanted to go home, but there was no way she could step foot in that house. When she looked at her brother Asa she could see he was just as anxious as she about going home.

"How about that kid?" asked Asa.

"Naah, too short. If he has to run he will be caught really fast," Tana pointed to another kid across the street. "How about him?"

Pumpkin knew this kid. "Heck no! He's scared of girls!"

"How about that guy? I see him at school. He's popular with all the kids at school, and he's big," Asa said impressed by his size.

"Yes, he is perfect. He seems like he would not be scared of anything. What's his name?" Tana asked.

"He's in tenth grade. I think his name is John, but everybody calls him Tank. You see he's built like one," Asa stated with awe.

"Yeah, he would be perfect! Now who's going to talk to him, and what story are you going to tell him?" Pumpkin asked.

"I say let Tana talk to him, because she's a girl. Tana could tell him, to tell whoever answers the door that he mows lawns, and wanted to know if they would be interested in have their lawn mowed. But she will tell Tank she just want to see if her dad's home. She has a gift she needs to bring into the house without dad noticing," said Asa.

"Now that's a plan! Here's my ten dollars. Just don't forget." Pumpkin reminded Tana in a warning tone.

"We know already!" Asa replied.

"I just want to make sure no one forgets." Pumpkin answered defensively.

Pumpkin hands over the money to Tana, and reminds her where the money came from.

"Okay Tana, go ahead," Asa said ignoring Pumpkin.

Tana walks across the street, and approaches Tank. Tana takes a deep breath and prays that this kid will do this, because the night was setting in, and she did not want to get caught out here in the dark. Putting on her innocent look, and little girl face for this kid name, 'Tank' she began to talk. She is seen by Asa and Pumpkin talking to Tank from a distance, and Tana pointing down the block towards her house.

Basil: "Boy oh boy. I can't wait to see what happens! That kid looks like he can eat a building!"

Tana is seen giving the money to Tank, she then turns to Pumpkin and Asa, and gives the thumbs up. She motions for them to follow her.

"Cool! Let's go!" Pumpkin yells while running.

They follow Tana and Tank from across the street, and hide in the bushes a block away about two houses down. Tana darts across the street running to Asa and Pumpkin before Tank reaches their house. Once Tank walks up the sidewalk the three of them are hiding. Tana noticed the windows in their house are different. That's when she realizes the blinds are drawn closed at every window. Tana knew their mom always had the curtains open, and the window shades were always up to let fresh air into the house. Tana was very nervous when she noticed this. Their windows were never closed she thought again. Asa turned and whispered to Tana.

"Looks like nobody is at home," Asa nervously pointed out.

Basil: "You think?"

As all three of them watch from the bushes Tank knocks on the door, then steps back. A few seconds later the door slowly opens. Because they are two houses down hiding behind bushes they could not see who opened the door inside the house. They all could see Tank back up slowly, turns tail and runs for his life the opposite way down the sidewalk. The door slowly closes. Asa, Tana, and Pumpkin sees this, and they run the other way down the street. They ran practically back to the other side of town, because they were so scared by what they saw. Even though none of them saw anyone in the house just the fact Tank turned and ran was enough to convince Tana and Asa they were not going home tonight. Tana was the first to stop, because she was fresh out of breath. As she leaned over with both her hands on her knees to hold herself up she was the first to speak.

"Okay, now I'm scared! What did he see?" asked Tana.

Asa was gasping for air so bad he could barely speak.

"I'm too scared to find out," said Asa.

"We have to find out. Let's go and find Tank. Come on!" Pumpkin urged.

Basil: "There they go! Just as clueless! Look at them run! Too bad they did not wait a little longer, because the curtains upstairs were moving."

They ran around town until they caught up with Tank around the corner bending down trying to catch his breath.

"What happen back there? What did you see?!!" asked Pumpkin.

"Nothing happened. I didn't see a thing," replied Tank.

"Really? Is that why you ran like your britches were on fire?" replied Pumpkin.

One thing Tank did not take kindly to, and that was being called a chicken by a snot nose kid. Heck, his dad was a cop, and he wanted to be a cop like his dad. There was no way he will let anyone know that he ran from anything. He was not going to take any lip from some bean pole, skinny kid. Tank looked Pumpkin straight in the eye with his fist ready to defend his honor.

"What did you say?" challenged Tank.

Pumpkin knew when he was licked as he backed up with his hands in the air as if he was being robbed.

"Hey, Tink," said Pumpkin.

"The name's TANK!"

Asa could not take it anymore, and he had to find out what did this kid see. He did not have time for Pumpkin needling this big kid, so he stepped up to Tank.

"Hey look Tank, you won't catch him. So don't bother. What happened back there?" Asa asked.

"I said nothing happened. I have to go. Leave me alone!" Tank said. Tank had enough with these three, plus he had to get home and help his mother plant some flowers in the garden. He stalks off in fear of what was in that house that could be coming after him.

"Aren't you guys going to stop him!" yelled Tana.

"Hey! What about my ten dollars?!! Why don't you stop him Asa!" yelled Pumpkin.

"I want to live. That boy is too big to mess with!" said Asa.

"I wonder what he saw," pondered Tana.

"Something really scary enough, to run home to his mama! Now what are we going to do?" asked Pumpkin. They all gave up, and sat on the curb trying to decide what to do next.

Basil: "Boy! I'm so mad I want to drink a pack of soda! Who was behind that door?!!! Or what was behind that door?!! Oh well, now what? Oh! Oh! Is that Uncle Marcus coming down the street? Yep! That's him!"

"Hey guys, what's going on? I went to the park, but I guess I missed your game Elliot. I'm sorry, but I had to finish work. Why are you three sitting on the curb like you lost your best friend?" asked Uncle Marcus.

Pumpkin looks at Asa for permission, and Asa nods his head 'no'.

"Oh, we're just bored," said Pumpkin.

Tana had her head down the entire time not seeing Asa and Pumpkin nodding not to talk about it to Uncle Marcus. She could not believe those two would sit there and say nothing is wrong, and at this point Tana swings her head up in shock about Pumpkin claiming he was bored.

"What? You call running from a crazy, creepy, looking guy is boredom!!!" yelled Tana.

"Whoa! Whoa! What guy? Who is chasing you? Where is this creep?!!" asked Uncle Marcus who suddenly became concern.

"It's not what you think. I mean this is not an ordinary guy," said Pumpkin.

"Okay look, I don't know what's going on here, but somebody needs to start talking. So, let me hear from someone what is this all about?" asked Uncle Marcus.

Pumpkin goes on to tell him the entire story with Tana and Asa filling in.

"Wow, that's some story. I have to say this is a little hard to believe," Uncle Marcus said.

"We are not lying!" Tana said.

"Okay, okay, I am not saying you are lying, but a man that floats, his face changes colors, and he appears at Pumpkin's bedroom window is really hard to believe," said Uncle Marcus.

"Uncle Marcus I'm not kidding! He had his face smashed up against the window!" exclaimed Pumpkin.

"Your bedroom is on the second floor," observed Uncle Marcus.

"I know! But he was there!" Pumpkin insisted.

"He was there, and I saw him up close!" yelled Asa.

"That is why I ran downstairs to get you and Dad!" Pumpkin explained.

"But Tana and Asa said they were playing. And don't you have a long ladder in the shed in back of the house? If there was someone that is what he would of used," said Uncle Marcus.

"Yeah," said Pumpkin.

"It's, yes," Tana corrected.

"Be quiet Tana, you said enough," said Asa.

"That could explain how he got up there if there was a man there," observed Uncle Marcus.

"I told you Pumpkin. Unless grownups can actually see things they will not believe you," said Asa.

"Hey, wait a minute," said Uncle Marcus.

With a sudden thought Pumpkin asked, "Wait! Could you take us to Tana and Asa's house? That will prove something is going on."

"Sure. Where do you two live?" asked Uncle Marcus.

"We live a few blocks away down the street, and around the corner," answered Asa.

"Well, let's go," said Uncle Marcus.

"Now, that's what I'm talking bout! Let's go!" urged Pumpkin.

Basil: "Whoa Nelly! Is that Pumpkin in the lead walking towards the unknown danger? Could it be he found some courage? Yeah right, we will see."

Walking through the neighborhood to Asa and Tana's house the kids go on to explain even further about the recent events with Scooter. When they reached their block Tana points out her house to Uncle Marcus.

"There's our house across the street," said Tana.

Pumpkin felt nervous. "I'll wait here just in case."

"Just in case what? So you can get a head start running?" asked Asa with a look on disgust on his face.

"Okay, that's enough you two. I want you all to wait here while I go knock on the door," said Uncle Marcus.

"Shouldn't we go get the cops or something?" asked Pumpkin.

Uncle Marcus smiled at his nephew quick idea, "I think I got this Pumpkin. If I see any sign of danger I will let you know."

"You don't have to tell Pumpkin, he will know when to go get help. Just watch him run," Tana said. Uncle Marcus headed across the street while the three kids argued among themselves.

"I saved you two! You probably would have been swallowed up by that one tooth creature if I didn't tell you to run," said Pumpkin.

Ignoring Pumpkin's bragging Asa notices what is going on across the street.

Nudging Tana Asa points, "Guys, look! He's knocking on the door!"

As Uncle Marcus knocks on the door the door slowly opens. He continues to knock leaning his head inside. He turns to the kids, and tells them to stay there as he goes inside.

"Pumpkin, what are you doing?" asked Asa.

Leaning over in a set position to run, Pumpkin did not want anything or anyone to catch him. He had to be ready to run for help, after all that was his uncle in that spooky house.

"I'm ready to run for the cops if anything weird comes out of there," said Pumpkin.

Tana felt guilty about Pumpkin's uncle in danger. "Do you think that thing is in there? Should we go in there after him?"

"Are you crazy?!!! That's my uncle, and he can handle anything. Besides, I am not going in there!" insisted Pumpkin.

"Well, if he does not come out soon then we need to go to the cops. We just can't stand here hoping he comes out," said Asa.

"I don't know if you guys noticed it, but that door was open when your uncle Marcus knocked on the door," said Tana.

Upon hearing this Pumpkin was ready to take a flying leap all the way home. He did not want to leave his uncle, but a kid had to do what needed to be done. That was getting help.

Basil: "Should we go or should we stay? He, he, he. Should we go or should we stay? Ho, ho, ho."

"Hey! There he is! Whew! I was beginning to wonder," said Asa.

Basil: "That was some kind of scary. Now what? Will he come back with a tooth, and some yellow pants?"

CHAPTER 10

Coming across the street towards the three scared stiff kids, Uncle Marcus crossed the street looking just fine. Pumpkin stands backing up in fear.

"Don't worry Pumpkin, I am not going to turn into anything, and I have all my teeth," Uncle Marcus smiled.

Pumpkin smiled with relief. "That's good. I could not bear having a one tooth uncle. What would mom and dad say?"

"What happened? Did you see anything?" asked Asa.

"Why was the door open?" asked Tana.

"Now wait minute guys, slow down. I walked inside and no one was in there. The door was unlocked, and I assumed your parents left it unlocked for you and Tana. I called around throughout the house and no one answered. When I went in the kitchen there was this note on the table. Here read it yourself," Uncle Marcus said. Uncle Marcus hands the note over to Asa who reads it out loud.

"Tana, Asa, dad and I are stuck out here just outside of Lincoln. The car broke down, and we are taking the car into the nearest mechanic shop. If we are not home by four I want you to stay over at your Aunt Gert's. I will call her and let her know you two are coming if we cannot make it back in time. Fix yourself and Tana a snack. If we cannot get home, make sure you lock the door behind you when you leave for Aunt Gert's. We will pick you up there. Love mom," Asa read.

"I don't want to go to Aunt Gert's! She will ask us how to use her computer, and then she will have us in bed by six! Remember the last time we were there? We had a bath, and the next thing you know she was saying lights out by five! It was still daylight out!!" cried Tana.

"Not only that, it was the summer time," said Asa.

Uncle Marcus could not believe these three kids, especially his nephew. He notice Tana and Asa was already talking about their parents note like everything was normal, even though they just called them monsters. Boy, he was not that bad when he was a kid he thought smiling from the memory. Well, let them have their fun of being scared.

"Okay guys. I have to do as your parents say. Let's get your things in the house to spend the night, because it is well past six. I will take you to your aunt's house," Uncle Marcus decided.

"I'm not going in there! Our house is spooky," Tana objected.

"I'll go," said Asa even though he was scared.

"I'll go with you, and help you pack what you need. Pumpkin you stay here with Tana," Uncle Marcus suggested.

"No problem uncle," said Pumpkin.

Basil: "HA! As if he needed to tell chicken Pumpkin to stay put."

Uncle Marcus and Asa heads across the street into the house.

"Well, I guess all we can do is sit and wait for them. I'm not going any closer, but if you want to, knock yourself out," said Pumpkin.

"Pumpkin, I have to agree with you on that one. I wonder what the inside of the house is like. I guess we will see very soon." Tana replied nervously watching her house.

"Where do you think your parents are Tana? I mean we both know you guys were at my house, and you did not hear from them, and that note didn't even ask about your night from home. What kind of parents do not ask about their kids not coming home."

"Creatures that are not your parents," replied Tana.

Pumpkin thought about something. "By the way, why don't you two have a cell phone?"

"Mom and dad think we're too young to have phones. Hey, Pumpkin?" whispered Tana.

"What?" Pumpkin answered with a tired look on his face.

"Who wrote that note?" asked Tana.

"I don't know Tana " Pumpkin replied.

"Asa and I cannot stay at our aunt's house. I think that thing would really get us, and our aunt would not know what to do, because she would be sound asleep in bed by six! We have to come up with why we have to be at your house tonight," said Tana.

"Well, you better think quickly, because here they come," Pumpkin responded getting up from the sidewalk.

Uncle Marcus and Asa crossed the street carrying bags over their shoulders walking towards them.

"Here's your bag Tana, I packed enough clothes for three nights. In the note mom says they might spend the night until the car is done, and it may take longer," said Asa.

Uncle Marcus could see everyone was tired. "Okay folks, there was no ghost in the house. It's getting late let's get going."

Basil: "Ha! That's what he thinks! Too bad they do not see those curtains moving upstairs."

"Oh wait! Uncle Marcus, Scooter's house is on the way. Can we stop by there to check in on him?" Pumpkin asked.

"That's right; he's the one in trouble as well. Okay, if that makes you feel better," Uncle Marcus assented. This quick thinking by Pumpkin make Asa see how good this kid was thinking on his feet. Asa had to admit Pumpkin always landed on his feet when his back was up against the wall. They all headed to Scooters house with their bags in tow. While walking behind his sister and Uncle Marcus, Asa hangs back talking to Pumpkin. He could see his sister talking uncle Marcus ear off.

"I hope you notice Pumpkin your uncle does not believe us," said Asa.

"Yeah. Maybe Scooter's face will change his mind when that door opens," Pumpkin had hoped.

Once they arrived to Scooter's house Pumpkin, Tana, and Asa were a little bolder approaching the door, and that's because they had an adult with them this time. For once thought Asa, someone will finally see what they saw and believe them. They all walked up to the door with Uncle Marcus standing in the back. Asa knocks on the door, and Mrs. Walker appears looking much nicer than before.

"Why hello again," answered Mrs. Walker.

Introducing himself Uncle Marcus smiled to Scooter's mom. "Hi. I am Elliot's uncle, and they wanted to see your son before we head home."

"I'm sorry, but Henry has not come home yet," Mrs. Walker replied.

The three kids take a quick look at each other at a loss for words.

"Can you tell him we stopped by," said Asa.

"Sure. It was nice meeting you all." She closes the door, and they all turn and walk away wondering what happened to Scooter.

Basil: "Oh where oh where has our little Scooter disappeared?"

"Okay you three let's go," ordered Uncle Marcus.

Basil: "Now poor Uncle Marcus is in it, but he doesn't believe them. Will the one tooth stranger show himself in front of a grown up? We shall see."

Walking the few blocks to their aunt's house calmed Tana down, but she was still shaky about their house looking empty. One question she asked to herself, 'where in the world was Scooter?' She could not tell what her brother was thinking about, because he was so busy flapping his gums with Pumpkin. Asa and Pumpkin whispered among themselves making bets on where Scooter could be. 'Thank goodness' thought Tana, they finally arrived to aunt Gert's house.

"Okay kids, where is your aunt's home?" asked Uncle Marcus.

Asa pointed. "That's the house there across the street."

"Let's go," replied Uncle Marcus.

All of them walk across the street to the house, and Tana knocks on the front door, but after a minute or two there was no answer.

"Well, it looks like they have to stay with us," Pumpkin smiled.

Suddenly, the door swings open and they all jump, even Uncle Marcus. Standing in the doorway is Aunt Gert looking tall and lean with bags under her arms, and her purse strapped across her chest like someone was going to snatch it. Aunt Gert was a little put out, because she did not expect to see her niece and nephew standing on her doorstep with company. She had a lot on her mind, and one thing was for sure she had to pick up her buddies Gloria, Mena, and that party animal Theresa. Aunt Gert was ready for fun. Looking at her two little relatives brought joy to her heart, but not now. Seeing the bags on their shoulders had her thinking her trip was doomed.

"Asa, Tana, what a lovely surprise! I did not know you were coming over, because I'm leaving for a bingo tournament in Freemont. Why do you have your bags with you? Is something wrong?" asked Aunt Gert.

"Nothing is wrong auntie, mom and dad's car broke down out of town, and she wants us to stay with you until they come back," Asa answered hoping his aunt will say, 'no.'

"Well that's a problem, because I am driving three other people who are going with me," said Aunt Gert.

"We can stay with Pumpkin tonight! His parents won't mind, because we stayed there last night!" Tana offered.

Aunt Gert turned and looked at the tall lanky kid standing shifting back and forth in the background.

"What kind of name is Pumpkin? What were your parents thinking?" inquired Aunt Gert.

Standing in the back Uncle Marcus smiled as he watched their aunt. Asa and Tana could see their aunt Gert had that busy look on her face. That was just perfect for them. Before Pumpkin could answer her, his uncle stepped in.

"Excuse me. My name is Marcus, and I am his uncle. His given name is Elliot, but the kids call him Pumpkin."

Aunt Gert was wondering who in the world would name their child Pumpkin. She also wondered what this world is coming to. Aunt Gert notice they were all staring at her, she figured she better get this situation straight, because she had somewhere to go.

"Oh," replied Aunt Gert.

"Ma'am, it is not a problem for them to stay with us. My sister knows their parents very well, and they spent the night like Tana said. We have the extra room," suggested Uncle Marcus.

"Well, I guess it's alright if they spend the night. Please tell your parents they need to get a doggone cell phone," chided Aunt Gert.

Asa became excited. He could see his Aunt Gert had no intention of missing the bingo game with her buddies. He knew is aunt loved them. She was always there for them if mom and dad needed her, but this is the one time he was glad his aunt was raring to go on her bingo trip.

"Sure Aunt Gert! We'll make sure we will tell them," Asa grinned.

"Let us help you with your bags!" Tana offered.

"Okay you two, I don't know why you are so excited, but I don't have time to figure out what is going on," said Aunt Gert.

Asa and Tana went down the driveway to help Aunt Gert load the car with her bags and waved goodbye, as she pulled out of the driveway. Asa yelled out to her waving goodbye with relief.

"Okay auntie, I will let them know! Have fun!" Asa yelled.

"Have a great time Aunt Gert!" Tana waved to the car.

"Well guys, what are we waiting for? I know there is dinner on the table waiting for us," Uncle Marcus mentioned.

"Yes there is, and I am ready to chow down!" exclaimed Pumpkin.

Basil: "Well, well, now we are one big happy family on our way to Pumpkin's house. Let's see how brave they really are."

After carrying bags and visiting Scooter's house and his aunt's house, Asa was ready for a good meal. He did not realize how hungry he was until he stepped through the front door of Pumpkin's house and smelled dinner. Tana was tired, but the smell of food perked her up as well. Pumpkin was hungry, as soon as they left the house early in the morning. Pumpkin was glad the day was over, but he needed to regroup after that scare with Scooter. The thought of looking at Scooter with one tooth made his knees shake. Pumpkin's mom and dad were happy to have Asa and Tana again, and told them to stay however long it was needed. Pumpkin was relieved and now the tiredness began to really set in once everyone was settled.

Pumpkin pulled his uncle to the side. "Uncle Marcus, are you going to tell mom and dad what we told you?"

"Only if you want me to," said Uncle Marcus.

Basil: "His uncle didn't believe him. Tisk, tisk. Does Pumpkin look sad or glad? Sad, because that means they are back on their own or glad cause Uncle Marcus cannot see a thing in those glasses anyway!"

Pumpkin could not believe what his uncle said which told him his uncle did not believe him. Pumpkin felt too tired to argue or even care at the moment.

"Come on guys, let's go upstairs to my room," said Pumpkin.

Uncle Marcus watched them head up the stairs "Elliot I will tell your parents that your friends will spend the night."

"Thanks, we will wash up for dinner," Pumpkin said quietly.

All three went into the room. Pumpkin layed on his bed tossing a ball in the air, Tana was sitting on the floor by the window, and Asa was sitting at the desk with the computer.

Tana was hesitant, but she had to ask. "Now what are we going to do? It sounds like your uncle does not believe us."

"Trust me, he does not believe us. Or else he would of ran in there and told mom and dad right away," Pumpkin answered quietly.

"I think you're right. I don't know about all of this, but it is getting weird. Remember, our so call mom and dad wanted us downstairs early to talk to us, and we took off in the morning and did not come home. They did not look for us, and I never talked to them when we got to Pumpkin's house later that day. Then they left a note for us to go to Aunt Gert's house," said Asa.

Pumpkin stared at Asa with fear in his eyes. "That tells me those are not your parents. And if they are not your parents, who are they?"

"What if we try and bring that thing to us?" asked Asa.

"What? Are you crazy?!!" said Tana.

"Hey, that's my line. Are you crazy? Even if we did that, what are you going to do?" You notice I said, *you*," Pumpkin pointed out.

"WE will do better if we strike first. I am getting tired of looking over my shoulder and waiting to see if he pops up on us Asa answered."

Tana agreed with her brother. "Yes, it is nerve racking,"

There was a knock at the door, which made them all go silent. Mom opened the door bringing in a tray of food.

"I decided to make hot dogs and burgers. I know you would rather eat with each other than us grown folks," Mom said.

"Thanks mom!" Pumpkin greedily replied looking at the food.

"Thanks Mrs. Smith!" Asa answered with a growling stomach.

Mrs. Smith handed over the tray of food. She could see the kids looked tired, but she was glad they were hungry and glad they stopped all the scary storytelling to each other. Now if only she could teach her son to clean his room.

"Enjoy. Make sure you bring the tray down when you are finished," Mom instructed.

"Okay mom," Pumpkin answered with a mouth full of food.

As soon as Pumpkin's mom left the room, Tana got down to business. She was ready for any kind of escape plan from the scary looking stranger. She also thought this was too much stress for a kid to handle. Tana could see her brother Asa was not looking any better. But this did not stop them from eating.

"Your mom is great, and thanks for letting us spend the night again. Well, what are we going to do?" asked Tana.

"What if we go back to the park? That is where he is. Why not confront him there?" suggested Asa.

"How many times am I going to ask you? Are you crazy? That thing floats. It's ugly in the worst way, and his face changes colors plus those big, old shoes. Face him and do what? We can't beat him. You see how tall he is!" Pumpkin said.

"Do you have any other ideas?" Asa questioned.

"What will we say or do? We just stand there ready for him to snatch us?" Tana wondered.

Asa was tired and ready for a plan. "How else do we go about it? Do you really want to wait and have this guy sneak up on us again and in the dark? If you noticed, Pumpkin lives on the edge of town, and there isn't any lights out here. If we do come up with an idea I rather we do this plan in the daylight at the park. I say we get to the park early in the afternoon instead of later in the day."

Pumpkin started thinking, "Do you think he will show up? It seems like he appears when it gets late in the day."

"When no one is around," added Tana.

"Well, let's try early in the day. If we have to then we wait it out at the park till late afternoon," said Asa.

"Once we see him, then what do we do is the question." asked Tana.

Pumpkin shook his head in disbelief. "Let me get this straight. We see him, and we stand there and ask him a question!! What else you got Sherlock? You can stand there, but I will not go to that park waiting for grizzly tooth to come and eat us!"

"Pumpkin, what else can we do? Can you go another night of him showing up at your window? It's getting dark, and I know I cannot take his face again," replied Asa.

"As scared as I am, I agree with Asa. We still don't know what happened to Scooter," observed Tana.

"Scooter! Let's call him! Let's confront him about what happened at the park. At least we are safe by calling him," said Pumpkin.

"Good idea!" Asa agreed.

Thinking they had a good idea they headed downstairs to the hall phone. Pumpkin dialed the number, as Asa and Tana waited behind him.

"Well, is it ringing?" asked Asa.

Pumpkin hung up the phone with a puzzled look on his face.

"It's ringing, but no one is answering the phone. That's strange," said Pumpkin.

"What's strange about the phone ringing?" wondered Tana.

"I could not leave a message. He has voice mail, and it did not come on," said Pumpkin.

Asa was confused. "What does that mean?"

"I don't know! All I do know is that his voicemail is not on. Scooter was proud of his voice message because he was able to clown around with it," noted Pumpkin.

Asa was not thrilled about his idea, but said it anyway. "Pumpkin, we have to go to his house tomorrow to see if he shows up."

"If he does not show up at home tonight don't you think his parents will call here? And if they don't call that means nothing happened," said Tana.

"I think you're right Tana. Any parent would look for their kid if they don't show up. If they can't find them, then they call their friends," said Asa.

"Well there is nothing else we can do until tomorrow. Wait a minute. Why don't I turn on the back porch light to keep that creep away from the house. The light will brighten up the entire backyard! Maybe he will think twice before he shows his face at my window again," Pumpkin bragged.

"That's a great idea," added Tana.

Basil: "Really, that's all you got?"

With pep in their step they all headed to the kitchen door and Pumpkin turned on the porch light. Standing inches from the glass door the strange looking man was standing there staring at them through the glass smiling with the one tooth. Pumpkin was so close to the window he saw every shape and ugly bumps on the strangers face. After getting an up close look at the guy they all screamed bloody murder.

CHAPTER 11

Pumpkin knocked over Asa and Tana running away from the door. Pumpkin's parents and Uncle Marcus came running into the kitchen. Mr. Smith was first into the kitchen tripping over Asa and Tana yelling at the kids what is going on, because he could not see a thing without his glasses.

"What's going on in here?" Mr. Smith demanded.

"What is all the screaming about? What are you kids doing?" Mom asked.

"Don't tell me you three are still at it," said Uncle Marcus.

"That thing was there at the door! Right Tana!" screamed Pumpkin.

"Yeah! The tooth was staring at us! And it was wet! Yuck!" Tana cringed.

"For once and for all, I will stop this nonsense. I'll go out and look for this monster," said Uncle Marcus.

"I'll go with you just in case," offered Mr. Smith.

"Be careful, and here are some flashlights" warned Mom.

While inside the kitchen they all watched, as Mr. Smith and Uncle Marcus unlocked the door and walked out into the backyard with flashlights shining around the trees and bushes. What they saw was Butch the dog tied up and barking his little head off. Once they thought it was safe Pumpkin's uncle and father came back into the house. Pumpkin could see their faces, and all hope of convincing them the creature was out there dashed his hopes. Everyone stood in the kitchen silently in their own thoughts. Finally, Pumpkin spoke up.

"So you really don't believe us," asked Pumpkin with a touch of bitterness.

"Elliot, there were times you stretched the truth, and lied to us, remember?" asked Mom.

"I know mom, but Asa and Tana saw him as well," Pumpkin replied.

"Didn't they say they were playing, and you told your uncle nothing was wrong when he saw you three outside on the sidewalk? Am I correct?" Mom asked.

"Well, yeah," said Pumpkin.

"You mean 'yes'," Mom said.

"Well, there is nothing out there, and the gate was locked just like I left it. Elliot you know to get in the backyard one has to come through the house, and you need at least a twenty foot ladder to go over the top of the fence. When you three were yelling we came in the kitchen within seconds. So how do you explain that?" Dad questioned.

"I don't know dad! But I'm telling the truth he was right there!" Pumpkin answered with frustration.

Basil: "Yeah up real close dad!!!"

Pumpkin's uncle could not figure out what his nephew was up to, and he knew Pumpkin had a way of stretching the truth to get out of doing things. Yet, he could not help but feel Pumpkin believed in what he was saying. To take the seriousness away from the night Uncle Marcus decided to make a little joke to make everyone feel a little more at ease.

"Unless he is a pole jumper without the pole," Uncle Marcus joked.

"Okay you three, that's enough excitement for the day. Go upstairs and get ready for bed. I will be in to check on you guys," Mom instructed.

Just to make the kids feel safe Mr. Smith stated, "I will check all the doors just to make sure they are locked."

Asa, Tana, and Pumpkin were so let down they went upstairs without another word. Once inside the bedroom they begin talking among themselves.

"How in the world did he disappear like that? That only took seconds! That's it! I'm covering my windows, because I don't want him snooping by my window again," Pumpkin replied.

"What do you have to block the window with?" asked Asa.

"I'm sure I'll find something," said Pumpkin. Pumpkin goes to his closet which is full of junk, and Asa helps him sift through the clothes on the floor.

"All you have in here is posters, shoes, and piles of clothes," observed Asa.

Tana looked about the room and had an idea. "Hey! How about these cinder blocks you have your books and stereo on."

Pumpkin felt Tana was a pain, but the girl had a plan. "Good idea! Let's start taking this stuff off and put it on the window sill."

Pumpkin's mom walks through the door while knocking.

"What are you three doing?" Mom asked.

"We are just cleaning up so Tana will have more room on the floor," Pumpkin answered with an innocent look on his face.

"Oh, I thought you were actually cleaning up the entire room. Well, good night and please keep it down in here. No more foolishness," Mom warned.

Once Pumpkin's mom left the room, they returned to piling the cinder blocks on the window sill.

"That was close. Come on guys; keep handing me the cinder blocks," said Asa.

Tana struggles and hands them the blocks to put on top of the bottom of the extra curtains material lying on the floor.

"Make sure your window is locked," said Tana.

"It's always locked. I never open the window," said Pumpkin.

"That explains the smell," Tana noted.

"That explains why I will tell you to go home!" retorted Pumpkin.

"Okay you guys, cut it out. Well, that's stacked high enough. I'm getting ready for bed," Asa replied.

"Me too," added Tana.

"Well, I guess we can't go any higher," said Pumpkin.

Asa stepped back and looked at the blocks stacked high in front of his window, now he felt a little safer. Asa thought if this creature tried getting through the window he would have to knock down all the cinder blocks before he could reach them. This made him feel a little bit better. Tana and Pumpkin liked the stacked wall they built as well. Once they prepared for bed, and put on their pajamas the excitement of the day began to wear them down. Lying down talking about what had happened did not make Asa feel any better, but he was glad him and his sister were not alone in this.

"Let's go to Scooter's house before we go to the park," said Asa.

"And do what? If he's there I'm not getting anywhere close to him!" Pumpkin chimed in.

"Hey, you know what? What did Scooter say when he turned around and looked at us in the park?" asked Tana.

"I don't know, because I was backing up, and staring at his gross face. I couldn't hear a thing after that," said Pumpkin.

Asa thought for a second. "I think he said, 'he wanted to ask us something.'"

Tana pondered. "I wonder what he wanted to ask us too."

"Sure Tana, why don't you head on over to his house, and ask him now. I'm sure he will tell you," Pumpkin smirked.

Tana laid in the dark thinking of going over to Scooter's house made her shudder with fright.

Basil: "There they go. They must have had a tiring day, because they are already in la la land sleeping."

An hour later Pumpkin's mom silently comes in to check on them while they are sleeping. She sees the stacked blocks on the curtain and smiles. She walks over to the window, and goes to pull back the curtain. She reaches for the curtain, and then changes her mind shaking her head whispering to herself.

"Now I'm beginning to believe them," said Mom. She smiles as she leaves the room. "What is wrong with me? What are they thinking about with these stories they make up?"

Basil: "Open that curtain and you will see!"

Tana wakes up the next morning and looks at the window and grins with excitement. She turns over and wakes up Asa and points to the window.

"Asa, Asa, wake up! I think we kept him out!" said Tana.

Asa was tired, and Tana was annoying him. "What is it Tana?"

He sits up rubbbing the morning sleep out of his eyes, and looks at the window where Tana is pointing, and Asa sighs with relief.

"I sure hope so," said Asa.

Asa gets up and walks over to Pumpkin, and shakes him awake. Wake up Pumpkin! Pumpkin sits straight up yelling for his mom.

"Wha, what!!!" exclaimed Pumpkin.

"Look! He didn't get through our blocks!" Tana pointed out.

When Pumpkin sees their cinder blocks were not moved he jumps out of bed, and gives Asa and Tana a high five.

"Yes!! Now we're talking! Let's go to the park and beat that thing!" said Pumpkin.

"Oh, aren't we brave," mocked Tana.

Basil: "A few concrete blocks and you three are ready to beat up the world!"

"Okay Tana, that's enough. We got to get dressed, and head for the park," said Asa.

"I am ready to eat! I am starving!" exclaimed Pumpkin.

After they got dressed, Asa was excited. Pumpkin was right there with him in the excitement department. They felt they had beaten this thing as they headed down to the kitchen for breakfast. Pumpkin's mom could see the difference in the kids this morning, and she was glad they decided to stop with the scary stories. She had enough to worry about. As she prepared breakfast she thought about Asa and Tana's parents.

"Asa, have you heard from your parents?" Mom asked.

Basil: "Hmmm, what will honest Abe say now? Will he tell the truth, or another stretch of the truth, okay, I mean lie?"

"Yes ma'am," whispered Asa.

Basil: "Look at them. Looks like Tana just swallowed a fish. He,he,he."

"They will spend another night there in town, because it has something to do with the car engine. She says to tell you 'thank you' for putting up with us," said Asa.

"Oh honey, you and your sister are a pleasure to have," said Mom.

Basil: "Boy his pants are burnin up from that big fat lie!"

"Stay as long as you need to. So what do you three plan on doing today?" asked Mom.

"We are going to hang out at the park. All the kids are getting on the new stuff out there," said Pumpkin.

"Well all of you should be very careful, and Pumpkin you know to be home before the street lights comes on," Mom added with note warning.

"I know mom," replied Pumpkin.

"It's only nine o clock in the morning. You want to be at the park for that long?" asked Mom.

"Yes Mrs. Smith. We have a lot of friends we hang out with there," added Tana.

Basil: "Sheesh! Her pants are really burning for that lie! This whole house should go up in flames from all this fibbing!!"

"Well, I will be out all day today with dad, and your uncle is downtown at work. I will see you all later," Mom said.

"Bye mom," Pumpkin grinned while hugging her.

"Be good Elliot," his mom warned.

"Yeah right!" Asa said.

Tana was so excited about beating the weird guy with the cinder blocks she forgot to correct Asa about saying,'yeah.'

"See you three later, and be good!" Dad chirped.

Pumpkin anxiously peeks around the kitchen corner as he watches his parents leave the house. Just to make sure they are gone, Tana runs past Pumpkin to the living room window, and watches as Pumpkin's parents back out of the driveway. Only when she sees them driving down the street she turns and yells to the others they are gone.

"Okay guys, let's do it!" as Pumpkin yells with excitement.

"Should we take anything with us to protect ourselves?" Asa asked.

"Sure Asa. Like a Beebe gun or I don't know a rocket blaster!" said Pumpkin.

"So we go empty handed?!!" Tana exclaimed.

"Yep! You two are related! That thing floats, looks through windows on the second floor, and faster than us! Duuuh! The only thing we can do is run, and hoping there are people around to help us," said Pumpkin.

"Monkey muffins!" shouted Asa.

"What did you say?" asked Pumpkin.

Tana sighs. "He says that when he is mad, and upset."

"Oookay. Let's go and get this over with," Pumpkin said.

"If we are going to Scooter's house first, I want to make sure my sneakers are tied tight when we are ready to run. Asa and I tripped over each other, and we could have been caught. Thank goodness it was his mother," Tana said.

"I think we should throw rocks at the door until somebody answers! That will do it," said Pumpkin.

"Even though that sounds crazy I like the idea. I don't want to get snatched by whoever is on the other side of that door. Let's go," said Asa.

"Oh wait! I forgot to feed Butch," said Pumpkin.

Tana groaned at Pumpkin's forgetfulness. "Hurry up!"

"Okay, okay." Pumpkin goes through the pantry, and finds the dog food to feed Butch. It being day time Pumpkin does not have any fear of seeing this guy, and there is no rain or storm outside. He unlocks the kitchen door to go and feed Butch, and then he yells for Asa and Tana to come outside. Pumpkin is standing by the dog house in shock.

"Asa! Tana! Come here! Quick! Look at this!" Hearing Pumpkin scream jolted Asa and Tana to run outside forgetting their fear of the stranger in the backyard. When they reach the yard they see Pumpkin pointing to the dog house. What Asa and Tana see is Butch tied up on the other side of the dog house jumping up and down with the huge foot prints heading out the backyard, and stops by the gate. Not only the sight of the huge footprints is scary, but the prints are on the gate door going up and over the top of the gate!

"He was here!" Asa yelled.

"You think!" mocked Pumpkin.

"Even though they are big these footprints are the size of a kid!" marveled Tana.

On the other side of the yard Pumpkin is jumping up and down yelling, and pointing towards footprints leading straight to the house underneath his window. The footprints were going straight up the side of the wall to Pumpkins window.

"Hey! Look at this!" shouted Pumpkin.

Basil: "Yikers!!"

"Whoever it is made it all the way to your window!" Tana observed.

"But they couldn't get in! Your window is still closed! Hey, wait a hot cotton picking minute, do you think it was Scooter?" Asa asked.

The three of them standing there staring at each other, but they could not move, they figured out what had happened,

Basil: "Look at the three little statues standing there."

"I don't know about you guys, but I am scared," said Pumpkin.

Basil: "Jeez Louise, Look at em. They look like three lost sheep, and there is no one there to point them in the right direction. Baa, Baa. Maybe they will figure this out, because I am tired of that tooth! NOT! Oh wait, wait! Tana is looking like she has a thought!"

"Hey, what happened to those footprints we saw the first time? Pumpkin, when your dad and uncle went in the backyard last night they did not mentioned anything about footprints?" said Tana.

"Then again, dad cannot see anything in the dark, even with his glasses on," said Pumpkin.

"Your uncle can't either, even when he wears glasses," said Asa.

Pumpkin, Asa, and Tana stood there staring at the footprints going up the side of the house. Now they really did not know what to think. "Maybe those footprints disappeared" Tana squeaked with fear.

"Or they came back and erased them," said Pumpkin with fright.

"Do you know how dumb that sounds?" Tana asked.

"Well Miss Know at All, how do you explain the missing footprints?" Pumpkin asked while they all stared at the locked gate.

"I can," answered the stranger.

CHAPTER 12

When they heard the slurping sound behind them they all turned to see the man with the fat hanging tooth standing there. He had on his yellow pants, long colorful coat, big huge shoes, a zig zag cane, and his unusual face constantly changing colors.

Basil: "He, he, he. Pumpkin so scared he forgot to run. I think his feet are glued to the ground!"

"Don't bother running, because you have nowhere to go. (Slurps) And there is no one here to help you. I will catch any of you this time, (slurps) because there is nowhere.... to run to," warned the Stranger.

Basil: "Look at the three of them backing up like they have somewhere to go. Run Pumpkin, run! Well, scream Tana, scream! Well, somebody do something!"

Asa was so scared he started stuttering.

"Wha, wha,what do you want?!!!" yelled Asa.

"Mommmmy! Daddy!" Pumpkin cried.

"No one's here, Pumpkin," said the Stranger.

"How,how,how do you know my name?" asked Pumpkin.

"I know all your names," slurped the Stanger.

"Where's Scooter?!!" asked Pumpkin.

"I have Scooter," said the Stranger (slurps). "Miss him? You three are coming with me."

Tana starts crying, and Pumpkin runs for the gate yelling for his parents. Asa stands there holding on to his sister wishing he had the courage to run behind him.

"Maaama! Uncle Marcus!" screamed Pumpkin.

Basil: "Didn't that thing say you guys are all alone! Boy they don't listen! Sheesh!"

Beckoning them with his finger for them to come closer made Asa ready to throw up his breakfast.

"Come closer," said the Stranger. (Slurp) "I have something to ask you three."

Asa and Tana backs up, and take off running next to Pumpkin who is clawing the gate to get out. The Stranger's big shoes flip flops on the ground coming closer. He gets up real close, and personal facing them when Pumpkin turns around to face him with his back up against the gate. This is when the Stranger slowly blows out air in their faces.

Basil: "Boy! I bet that stinks! Look how they just dropped like flies."

All three of them had fainted. Not knowing what just happened, and feeling as if he blinked, Asa had found himself standing looking at Tana and Pumpkin. Not only were they confused standing facing each other, but they saw they were in a in a wide open clearing in the dead of night. They can barely see each other, as each of them began spinning around in circles with no one moving.

"What happened? Where are we? It's pitch black out here!!!" exclaimed Pumpkin.

"We were in the backyard! How did we end up here?!" pondered Tana.

"I don't know, but there's a bus over there," replied Asa.

The yellow school bus stood a few feet away with its doors open, and its engine revving. Not one of them moved an inch from their spot.

Basil: "Where's that courage?"

You can call it fear, because the three stood there watching the bus with only the headlights shining. The bus was revving its engine, like it was telling them to get on the bus. Asa thought the bus sounded mad, he could feel it was telling them to hurry, and get on the bus. The doors continued to open and close.

Basil: "The bus is ready guys, what are you waiting for? I would get on it before something bad happens."

The bus revs its engines even louder, with the doors moving.

Basil: "GET ON THE BUS!!"

"Why do I feel like it's waiting for us?" asked Pumpkin.

Basil: "BECAUSE IT IS!!!"

"I'm not getting on there. I don't see a driver!" said Tana.

The bus closes its doors and takes off without them swallowed up in the dark night. They could hear the rustling of trees behind them, but when they turn around they do not see anything there. Asa, Tana, and even Pumpkin hugged each other, because they were so scared.

"What was that Asa?" asked Tana.

"I don't know Tana. But it sounds awfully close," Asa replied.

"You think! It's coming through the trees," said Pumpkin.

"But there are no trees out here!" shouted Tana.

With the three of them holding on to each other they slowly start backing up from the departed bus. When Pumpkin turn to run there is a subway car waiting with the doors open.

"For some reason I think we are supposed to get on," said Pumpkin.

"Look, it's not touching the ground!!!!" exclaimed Tana.

"I think we better get on. I don't want to stand here," said Asa.

The subway doors started closing very slowly, and that's when they decided to make a run for the train. No sooner than they ran on the subway, the doors slam shut. Looking throughout the subway, they could see there is only one pole throughout the entire car, and they run to it and held on. The subway car takes off speeding through the pitch-black night, jostling them back and forth. Inside the subway, it is dim, but not so dark where they could still see each other. There were no seats to sit down, just one big space with large windows.

"Where is he? Where is yucky tooth? One minute we are safe in my backyard, and now we are on a subway speeding through... what?!!!" Pumpkin said. Sheer panic is on Pumpkin's face, and he shows every bit of it by the look on his face. His lower lip is trembling.

"Wait, how does a subway car make the noise of a train whistle?!! I can't see anything outside the windows," cried Tana.

"I don't think I want to see anything," said Pumpkin.

Asa looked around in full fear. "Me either."

The train car bumps them around, and the sounds are like they are going through trees in a forest. It was the sound of trees in a forest hitting the windows as they sped by.

Basil: "Hold on folks! I told you this will be one bumpy ride!! Weeeee!!"

Pumpkin turns around holding on to the pole looking down at the end of the train. As Pumpkin held on to the pole he is squinting to get a better look at the end of the train car. He is not sure, but he thinks he sees something at the end of the train. He can barely make it out because of the shadowy darkness.

"Hey guys, is that someone down there?" asked Pumpkin.

Tana spins around with Asa.

"Where?" Tana asked with a trembling voice.

All Pumpkin could do was point, because the cat had got his tongue.

"Right there!" yelled Asa.

Basil: "Can one say: Scarrrry."

They can barely make out a figure that is standing there at the end of the train car. It's a tall, shadowy figure, heading straight towards their way. They cannot tell if it's a teenager, or a kid. Asa yells at the shadowy figure.

"Who are you?!! Can you help us?!!" Asa asked.

All they hear is a slurping sound.

"Eeeww," Tana screams.

"Did you guys hear that?!!! It slurped!!!! Its Yuck Tooth's relative!!" yelled Pumpkin.

The shadowy figure limps faster towards them, but suddenly the train comes to a screeching halt throwing everyone to the floor, and the doors slowly open. The subway whistle blows, and all three kids are still on the floor. They are looking for the figure at the end of the train. The shadowy figure gets up coming towards them.

Basil: "I think it's time to get off."

"It's coming at us! Who are you?!" shouted Asa.

Basil: "Monkey muffins, monkey's uncle! Who cares! GET OFF THE TRAIN!"

The whistle blows again even louder than before.

Basil: "GET OFF!"

"It's running to us!" Tana yelled.

"Run!!" yelled Pumpkin.

The doors were slowly closing, but they made a mad dash through the closing doors off the train. In one swift motion the doors slam shut. As the train slowly pulls out, all they can see is a pair of hands flat up against the window. The train sprints out into the thick forest. The three of them are standing there staring at the forest where the train had been hearing only the sound of the whistle.

Basil: "Sheesh! Talk about slow!"

"I think I have to go to the bathroom," said Pumpkin.

Basil: "Me too!! Geez Louise!!"

"Figures. Not so fast guys, look around you " whispered Tana.

Standing there they all turn to see the thick forest with tall trees surrounding every inch of space. The trees are so tall it just about blocks out the sunlight.

"Well, I would think with all these trees I will have some privacy," said Pumpkin.

Squirming, he goes behind the nearest tree to go to the bathroom while Asa and Tana are talking.

"I can't believe this is happening to us. Nothing makes sense. A subway car with a train whistle, a kid on the train alone, moving bus with no driver, and going through trees that don't exist!" said Asa.

"I feel like we are in the movies, but we are the movie! That train ride was down, right creepy, and scary. Or was it the subway? Who was that Asa?" Tana asked.

After Pumpkin was through, he joined the conversation hoping to cover up his fear.

"Who knows Tana? Speaking of movies, have you ever notice no one ever has to go to the bathroom," asked Pumpkin.

"Seriously? Is that really what you are worried about?" Tana asked with anger.

Pumpkin had enough of Tana's 'I think I'm better and smarter attitude'. So, he decided to mock her by repeating what she said in a high pitch voice like an old lady.

"Seriously! Is that all you are worried about?" mocked Pumpkin.

It felt good to tease Tana, Pumpkin knew she hated when he did that to her.

"Quit it guys," Asa scolded.

"Ah come on. You have to admit no one ever eats, or have to go in the scary movies! By the way, that's the last time I will tell you two to run. You asked that thing at the end of the train, "who are you?"!! This ain't the movies! You two would still be on there carrying on a conversation with that thing. It's probably wet tooth's relative for all we know," said Pumpkin.

"Okay Pumpkin, let's go," Asa instructed.

"Go where? You act like you know where you are going," said Pumpkin.

"No! But we sure can't stand here all day, now can we!" said Asa.

Everyone was shell shocked of what just happened to them, but they all started walking, and within seconds they hear something behind them. Even though they heard movement behind them they began to walk a little faster.

"Is it me, or do I hear something walking behind us?" asked Pumpkin who refuse to turn around.

"I hear something walking behind us," Tana stated.

CHAPTER 13

"The one time I agree with you, and I am happy about that. I thought we were the only ones here," said Pumpkin.

They all turn to see what it is, and it's the Stranger at a distance floating. Pumpkin leans over towards Asa and whispers.

"I guess running is out of the question," said Pumpkin.

"Yes (slurps), running is out of the question, and you would not survive if you did. I've been waiting for you three," said the Stranger.

"Why is he so far away?" Tana questioned.

Hissing under his breath Pumpkin turned to Tana.

Ready to wring her neck, Pumpkin hisses, and whispers, "What is wrong with you? You want another good look up close?"

"Can't you hear me?" asked the Stranger.

"Yes! Yes! We can hear you loud and clear! You can stay right where you are!" warned Pumpkin.

"Who are you? What do you want!" asked Asa.

"I need your help," slurped the Stranger.

"Wait a minute, you can float, turn colors, peek in windows from the **second floor**, and you need our help! Why us?!" asked Pumpkin.

"I need kids," said the Stranger, (slurps) "and because you three like to lie... a lot."

"All kids lie! How are we any different?!" Asa replied.

"You never listen to your parents, and you make up stories when you should tell the truth," the Stranger said. (Slurps) "Now your parents will think you are running around not listening again. I left a note for your parents Pumpkin. It tells them Tana and Asa's parents are back, and you are spending the night with them. So you made it even easier to disappear. Look what happens when you lie all the time."

"You stole us because we lie!!!! I don't lie all the time!" yelled Pumpkin.

Basil: "Naah, MOST of the time."

"What do you want with us?!!" asked Asa.

"I" (slurps) "was with a traveling circus, and I was left behind. I need to find my way back," said the Stranger.

Leaning over whispering to Asa Pumpkin had to say it.

"That explains those pants, and face," said Pumpkin.

"And the shoes," whispered Tana.

"Are you two (slurps) finish? I need to get back with my circus, but I cannot do it without kids (slurps). Kids like the circus, and they know where to find them," said the Stranger.

Even though Pumpkin was scared out of his mind, he still put in his two cents.

"Why didn't you ask a grown up"? I don't know, they have cars to get you where you want to go! A GPS will do the job too!" observed Pumpkin.

"Once a grown up as you call them sees me then I would be a freak show for them," (slurps) "and they would want to try and figure out who I am, and stop me. They would" (slurps) "try and take me away, and I would not be able to get back to my circus," explained the Stranger.

"Why did you kidnap us?" Asa asked.

"Why not you?" slurped the Stranger.

"Where is Scooter?" asked Pumpkin.

"Your friend" (slurps) "is right behind you," said the Stranger.

Together they all spun around to find Scooter standing at a distance in the trees. Tana turns her back to Scooter facing the Stranger, only to find him only two feet away. She jumps, and lets out a little cry. When Asa and Pumpkin turns from Scooter they both jump back.

Tana was not so thrill looking at this man with one tooth, but she had to ask.

"Why is he standing there?" asked Tana.

"How do we know if that is really Scooter?" wondered Pumpkin.

"Call him," slurped the Stranger.

Pumpkin spins back around and hesitantly calls his friend while Asa and Tana anxiously watch.

"Scooter!" Pumpkin calls.

"Pumpkin? Is that you?" Scooter yells back.

"It's me, Asa, and Tana" Pumpkin yelled with fear.

Scooter starts towards them.

"Wait!! Do you have only one tooth in your mouth?" asked Pumpkin.

Confused, he stops and puts his hand to his mouth.

"No!!" Scooter yelled back.

"Okay!! Come on!!" said Pumpkin.

Scooter runs towards them, but he slows up a few feet keeping the distance between them. They all stand there staring at each other with many questions.

"Is it really you?" asked Asa.

"Yeah it's me lame brain!!" Scooter snapped.

"Yeah, it's him," Pumpkin gladly shaking his head.

"See why I picked him," observed the Stranger.

"Because he's mean?" said Tana.

"And a bully?" questioned Asa.

"Who's going to" (slurps) "miss a mean bully?" asked the Stranger.

"My parent's, that's who!" Scooter yells.

Scooter's feelings were so hurt he forgot about being scared.

"What happened to Scooter's one tooth?" asked Pumpkin.

"I don't need him anymore. Now he is back to being himself," said the Stranger.

"You mean having one tooth gives you powers?" asked Asa.

"I" (slurps) "needed him to bring you to me," explained the Stranger.

"How was he able to hide his tooth when we saw him?" Tana asked.

"I can do a lot of things. I needed to get you three, without anyone noticing what was going on" (slurps). "You three were too fast for him. That's when he had to come back to me. Yes, that was Scooter at your backyard trying to get through your window," said the Stranger.

"I knew it! That's why he wanted to ask us a question at the park before we ran, so he could breathe on us to knock us out!" yelled Pumpkin proudly figuring out he was right after all.

"My, my," slurped the Stranger. "Aren't we the smart one?"

Basil: "Naah, I wouldn't say smart, fast one, but not smart!"

Asa had a nagging question he needed to ask this guy, and with Pumpkin running his mouth it gave him a chance to build up his courage.

"Where are my parents?" Asa asked.

"Time to go," slurped the Stranger.

The Stranger turns his back on the kids and starts walking ahead.

"Go where? There is nothing but trees out here!!! There cannot be a circus here!" Asa exclaimed.

"Let's go," the Stranger repeated.

"How are we supposed to find a circus? We are in the middle of a forest!!" Pumpkin yelled with shock.

"How do we know where we are supposed to look?" asked Tana.

"We will not be in this forest (slurps) for long. Start walking, if you stop things will happen," warned the Stranger.

This caught their attention, which is why they began walking a little faster.

"What kind of things?" Asa asked.

Basil: "There he goes again, asking questions!"

"Keep standing there and you will find out," replied the Stranger.

The Stranger continues walking, and they continue to run behind him at a distance. They did not turn around for fear something would sneak up and snatch them. Little did they know the forest was rapidly disappearing behind them . Tana looked up at the tall, thick trees reminding her of the beautiful forest in California they visited on vacation, but she had an uneasy feeling about this so call forest. Something was not right.

"Don't stop guys," said Tana.

"You think!" mocked Pumpkin.

As they continue to walk Asa was itching to talk to Scooter. He thought Scooter looked the same, and acted the same, which was being mean. Practically running a short distance behind the Stranger Asa could not wait any longer to find out about what happened to Scooter.

"Scooter, what happened? Do you remember anything?" asked Asa.

"Yeah! Don't tell us you don't have a clue again!" said Pumpkin.

"I give up with you and the English language," Tana said.

"Sure Tana, I'm sure that's really important right now," said Pumpkin.

"He's right Tana. Let Scooter speak," said Asa.

"All I know is I was at home, and there was a knock at the door. When I went to answer it he pointed to the Stranger ahead of them was standing there staring at me," stated Scooter.

Basil: "Yeah, up close and personal!!"

"Next thing I knew I was standing here in the woods," Scooter said.

Chapter 14

"So, we are right back to where we were before, totally clueless on how we got here," said Tana. None of them notice, but they are beginning to lag behind seeing they were so busy trying to find out what happened to their friend Scooter.

"I think we should... Hey!!" said Pumpkin. Pumpkin begins swinging and flailing with his arms above him. He could feel something sharp over his head. If felt like a steel grip hand grabbing his head. "What was that touching my head?!!! My head was being squeezed!!"

"I told you things will happen if you don't start moving. Move!!!" yelled the Stranger.

All four of them started catching up by running, but keeping a safe distance.

Basil: "As if you had to tell them twice!!"

"Oh gracious I am scared Asa. How are we going to get back home?" asked Tana.

"I don't know Tana, but we will figure it out. Don't give up," said Asa.

"Keep walking, they are starting to catch up," the Stranger warned.

"Who, who, is starting to catch up?" asked Pumpkin.

"The Snatcher Catchers. If you stay still, you will see, and feel them." (slurps) "They will do worse than squeeze that big head of yours," said the Stranger.

Hearing his head was big really made Pumpkin mad, especially coming from a guy with one ugly looking tooth in his mouth.

"My head is not big!!" replied Pumpkin.

"Great Pumpkin, just argue with him. We don't have a choice but to follow him! Come on!!!" said Scooter.

Without turning around and walking at a hurried pace, the Stranger responded to Pumpkin without stopping.

"I would listen to your friend if I were you." (Slurps) "I can always go back and find more kids. Take me to my circus, and I will let you three go," offered the Stranger.

"How are we supposed to do that?" asked Asa.

The Stranger some feet ahead suddenly turns around and confronts them, the four of them collide into each other backing away.

"I don't know," (slurps) "but I am sure you will figure it out!!! You managed" (slurps) "to avoid me catching you for a few days, so I am sure you will be able to get me back to my circus," the Stranger answered.

The Stranger looks past the kids scanning his eyes around the forest, and without uttering another word he turns back around, and continues walking ahead of them.

Basil: "I guess he told them!! He, he, he."

"Guys, if we don't keep walking he will leave us," Scooter said.

"How do you know?" asked Pumpkin.

"Didn't he say he will get other kids?" said Tana.

"Okay, okay!" said Pumpkin. Pumpkin thought he heard something behind him; he stops and turns around to see the forest disappearing behind them. "Guys look! The forest is gone! Look!"

Asa, Tana, and Scooter stop to see what Pumpkin was pointing at.

"This is totally crazy," Scooter said.

"How in the world does a forest disappear?" Tana said.

"Or have a bus disappear into the night? Where are we?" asked Asa with a trembling voice.

"This place is nothing I studied in school, that's for sure!" said Tana.

"Or, that subway with the kid riding on it. It doesn't make sense for a subway car to blow a train whistle," said Asa.

"There is nowhere in the history books that a place like this exist with all these weird things happening," said Pumpkin.

"Unless, we are in another state! Think about it! What kind of circus would have this guy?!!" suggested Asa.

"A freaky carnival! That's who!" said Pumpkin.

"What do you think he is in the circus?!! Don't you think we would have heard of his floating," asked Asa.

"Yeah! Or we would have heard about his hot breath blowing you away! It knocked us all out!" chimed in Pumpkin.

The four of them stood in the middle of the forest in awe of how big the trees stood, and how there was something eerie about this beautiful forest. That's what made it even creepier.

"I don't think we are in a National Park. I'm telling you guys there is something strange about this forest!" said Tana.

He continues to walk ahead of them not turning around with the kids following him.

"You are right," said the Stranger.

"Right, right about what? It being a National Park or you have a weird circus you want to get back to?" asked Pumpkin.

"Both. Keep walking. Just because I'm different does not mean I'm weird. Welcome to my world," said the Stranger.

Scooter had had enough. He had a sloppy tooth in his mouth which did not feel good, and he did not like being kidnapped by a weirdo.

"I want to go home," Scooter whined.

"So do we Scooter. So do we," said Asa.

"Your world? Then how can we help you?" Pumpkin asked.

"There's not much time, keep walking, or you will not make it out of here," stated the Stranger.

Pumpkin thought whatever was behind them was ready to eat them for a snack, so he did not have to be told twice to pick up their slow speed.

"Maybe we are in the woods of Canada!" exclaimed Tana.

"Are you crazy? We could not travel that far that fast!!!" Pumpkin hollered.

Suddenly they all stepped through the clearing, and all they could see was nothing but open like desert with reddish sand for the desert floor. There were sand dunes, valleys, craters, and a mountain in the far off distance. The four of them could see they were standing at the edge of the forest looking down on a hill below. Tana could see there was space between where they are standing on the forest floor, and the sandy desert floor. She looked back behind them and saw the forest vanishing quickly behind them.

"This forest we are standing in is a floating planet," the Stranger explained.

The Stranger turns around and looks at them with that same dull look on his face. The kids are looking around at the desert in front of them.

"What happened?" Scooter yelled at anyone who would listened.

"Are you kidding? Where are we?" Pumpkin asked.

"If you are smart you will jump down onto this hill, and if you don't you will be lost in the forest forever. Just like the boy on the train you left. He would not listen to me," said the Stranger.

The Stranger turns around and floats down to the hill. The three of them look at each other and the forest disappearing behind them with long hands reaching out for their heads.

Basil: "Are you kidding! Are they going to just stand there?!! I give up!!"

All three turn to look at the disappearing forest. Pumpkin turns forward and jumps down to the hill with the other three following. They end up falling and rolling down the steep hill of sand.

Basil: "What? No questions this time?!! Now they're learning."

CHAPTER 15

After falling, and rolling down the hill they dust themselves off, but they have the fine, red dirt from the sand all over them. They all turn to look up and there is nothing but hands reaching from above. The Stranger is ahead of them, and he turns around.

"The 'Snatcher Catchers' are not fun to be with. They cannot bother you when I am around. That boy on the train did not listen," the Stranger repeated.

"We remember, so he rides the train?" asked Pumpkin.

"All day?" asked Scooter.

"He didn't listen, and that is how he got caught," the Stranger repeated.

"Can't he get off the train?" asked Tana

"No," the Stranger replied.

Hearing a sucking noise behind them, all the kids' turn around and look up to see the hands and forest disappear by being sucked into nothing but thin air. The top of the hill disappears in the desert. The Stranger turns and keeps walking.

"We are wasting time, let's go," the Stranger commanded.

All three are running behind him at a distance.

"Excuse me! There is nothing out here! We are going to die out here! This is the desert!" hollered Scooter.

"Excuse me! You cannot find your circus! Oh I don't know, but you think you can see it from here! In the empty I don't know, desert!!" Pumpkin yelled.

Exasperated, he spins around and quietly speaks in a menacing tone. Looking at his face, the kids back up stumbling over each other trying to keep a good distance from him.

"Yes this is another place. Yes this is the desert. Look around you, and you should be able to figure out where you are. Look at the dirt. The valleys, the craters, did you not learn anything in your schools?" asked the Stranger.

All four of them look around at their bleak surroundings.

"Is it Las Vegas?" asked Scooter.

The Stranger looks at Scooter with a confused look. He thinks how these kids could not know where they are was pathetic. Pumpkin interrupts the Stranger's thought with his answer on where he thinks they are. Pumpkin continues looking out at the landscape of the desert.

"Is this Death Valley?" Pumpkin inquired.

Exasperated the Stranger raises his arm, and points in the opposite direction. "Look."

Awed, and pointing in disbelief Tana think she figured it out, but she could not believe it.

"Is, is,is that, that,that what I think it is?" sputtered Tana.

She looks at the Stranger, then out past the empty desert, and back at the Stranger. Scooter could not believe what is going on, and all he wanted to do was go home. He felt he has not had a good day in a long time. This was all too much for Scooter, and even though he did not have a clue where they were he starts crying and really bawling like a new born baby.

"I want to go home!! I want my mommy, now!!" whined Scooter.

Basil: "Oh wait, is this our big, bad bully Scoot, Scoot, Scooter crying?!!"

All three were in too much of a shock to watch Scooter crying. Not believing what he sees, Pumpkin puts his hand on his hip pointing out in the distance.

"Aahh, get outta here. How did you do this trick? Ah come on guys he is from the circus!" said Pumpkin. Pumpkin is visibly shaking as he fumbles in his pocket for his cell phone and dials home with shaky fingers. He turns and looks at the others while he is dialing, and yelling, 'hello, hello' into the phone. The Stranger is staring at him with a straight face, and after a few yells of 'hello' into his phone, Pumpkin finally realizes it is true. "Are you, you crazy!! You took us from earth to, to..."

The entire time Asa stood there in a complete shock, but quietly finishing Pumpkin's sentence.

"Mars, the fourth planet from the sun," Asa said. Pausing, Asa continues giving information about the planet they are standing on. "It is also known as the 'Red Planet' because of its fine red sand."

"Red planet! What red planet? What red sand?!!" asked Pumpkin.

In a daze Asa answers Pumpkin's questions. Asa could not believe where they were, but he was excited to be there standing on the planet Mars.

"It's call the "Red Planet" because it gets its nickname for the fine, red dust that covers the surface," said Asa.

They all look at their clothes, which were covered in fine red dirt when they ran down the hill from the floating planet.

"You brought us to Mars! Whoa Nelly! Mars? No way! This is all a dream! No! A nightmare!! We are not on another planet! This, this ... is crazy!" yelled Pumpkin as he stares at the planet Earth.

Basil: "The word I'm looking for is, ummm, kidnapped!"

"Did you not say you want a one way ticket to Mars?" the Stranger asked.

Pumpkin, Asa, and Tana were stun, they knew Pumpkin made that comment, but the Stranger was nowhere around when he made that comment.

"How did you know that? You were not with us when I said that, and I was kidding!" said Pumpkin. Everyone was quietly staring off in the distance, until their attention turned and focus on looking at the Stranger.

"No one lives on Mars," said Asa.

"We do. And your kind will be here by 2037. We must get going elsc we could end up in a dust storm," warned the Stranger.

Pumpkin was beside himself with fear, and mentioning the word 'we' with this Stranger made him want to gag. "Why do you keep saying, 'we'?"

Ignoring Pumpkin the Stranger continued speaking.

"If that happens we can lose each other. We have to get to the cave. Don't try and run, the air is too thin for you humans for now. The danger in the forest is over," said the Stranger.

He turns and starts walking, but the four kids are still standing there in shock as the Stranger walks away. Pumpkin was still stuck on the word 'humans'. He started thinking if they were humans, then what in the world was he? Finally, after a few seconds the Stranger turns and sees they are still standing in the same spot where he left them. With mounting frustration he yells back at the three of them.

"Move!" yelled the Stranger.

That did not take long for all three to start running behind him, but keeping a little distance. After all, they still could not figure out what he was.

Basil: Can one say, "Help"!!!!!

TO BE CONTINUED...

Check my website for the next adventure
of Asa, Tana, and Pumpkin.

LTANYALEONE.COM

Made in the USA
San Bernardino, CA
19 January 2017